Dead Relatives

A Poppy Lewis Mystery

Book 4

Lucinda Harrison

Dead Relatives

ISBN: 978-1-7367596-3-9

One

I PERCHED ON the diner stool, still wrapped in my heavy jacket, and closed my eyes as I sipped my first glorious drop of coffee that day.

"Nothing like that first sip on a cold morning, is there, dearie?"

I nestled the mug in both hands and let a satisfied smile spread across my face. "No, Shelby, there sure isn't."

"You planning on breakfast, too?"

I glanced at the menu board on the wall peeking out behind her silver beehive hairdo. Shelby Shepard, owner of Shelby's Diner in our little haven of Starry Cove, stood erect with her free hand on her hip. The other held her ubiquitous coffee pot, ready to refill any mug that fell even an inch below the rim.

But before I could decide, the door swung open, letting in a waft of chilly morning air. Lovie Newman, wrapped in layers of cozy sweaters and scarves, barged in like a dolled-up tornado. She must have freshly applied her red lipstick because a few strands of her gray-blonde curls stuck to her lips. She spit them out in a huff. "Shelby," she said urgently, "you'll never guess what I just found out."

Shelby leaned in eagerly. "What, dearie? Spill it."

Lovie spared me one glance, then turned back to Shelby. "You didn't hear this from me, but guess who's coming back to Starry Cove?" This was a rhetorical question, of course, because she then said in the same breath, without pause, "Jim Thornen."

Shelby gaped. "I thought he was done with Starry Cove for sure, especially after losing the mayor's race. What's he back here for?"

Lovie flipped her hair, using the opportunity to give me a sidelong look, probably to make sure I was listening. "Apparently, he's got a new job. Something that puts him right in the thick of town business." She paused and looked around, feigning discretion. "I've said too much already."

"You want coffee then, dearie?"

"Yes, please," Lovie said. "I've got a long day ahead of me."

A long day of spreading rumors, I thought with a grin. Typical Lovie. She knew I was friends with the new town mayor, and Jim Thornen was a pebble I didn't need in my shoe. But she wasn't going to spoil the enjoyment of one of life's greatest gifts—hot coffee. I took another long sip, savoring the taste.

Shelby's voice brought me back. "You decide what you want yet, dearie?"

I took only a moment to decide on the French toast, but as I opened my mouth to order, the faint, yet distinct, sputtering of an engine caused me to pause. As the sound grew louder, a hair-raising cackle cut the air and drowned out the sound of the engine. Swiveling in the chair at the counter, I stared out the diner's large picture window, waiting with dread for the familiar scene to play out once again.

The hacking laughter crescendoed as a bright blue motor scooter appeared from the right and careened past the diner at the devil's pace. Atop it sat a tiny woman bundled in a puffy winter jacket like a marshmallow, clutching the steering bars in a death grip. She sped down Main Street with a banshee wail. A pair of driving goggles obscured her exuberant face, but I knew exactly who she was. So did everyone else.

"Uh oh, Poppy," Lovie said with a smirk. "Looks like your housekeeper's out for another joy ride."

Sighing, I set down my mug. "Sorry Shelby, but I've got to catch her. No breakfast for me."

Shelby nodded knowingly and her towering hair wobbled. "Sure thing. Coffee's on the house, dearie."

I thanked her and rushed out of the diner. Turning to my left, I spied the housekeeper and cook of my bed-and-breakfast already past the church and headed toward the narrow road that led down to the rocky shoreline. Long, gray hair trailed in the wind as she sped down the street. I raced after her along the sidewalk, my breath clouding with every stride, thankful I'd chosen sneakers with my overalls that morning instead of clunky boots.

As I passed the church, Pastor Basil Meyers sat on his meditation bench in the churchyard and squinted through his rounded glasses, then waved. "Blessed morning to you, Poppy."

I waved back, but did not slow my step. Greta would be close to the end of Main Street and too close to the cliff for my liking. I had to catch up.

Thankfully, the sound of the engine had died down, and I soon arrived at the end of the road. At this early hour, the fog that still hung heavy in the air obscured the view from this point to the coastline below the cliff. Greta had hopped off the scooter and stood silently staring into the hazy distance.

She pulled off the elastic band of her goggles with a snap. "Too much fog," she said in a ragged voice.

"Just what do you think you're doing?" I demanded, doubling over and wincing from a stitch in my side. "What did I say about taking my scooter out without asking?"

"I did ask."

"When?"

"The other day. I distinctly remember saying, 'I sure would like to get out of this dungeon and ride down and see the water.' Then I asked, 'Wouldn't you?' and you responded, 'Yes.'"

"That was three days ago," I said, heaving to catch my breath. "And you're taking my response totally out of context."

Greta shrugged. "Suit yourself."

"You remember what today is, right?"

Greta didn't respond.

"It's our grand-opening. Our first *real* guests. Guests whose checks won't bounce."

The old woman cut in curtly, "I told you that last group was trouble."

I waved a hand to silence her. I wasn't going to let

her change the subject on me. I'd worked too hard to renovate and prepare my late uncle's Victorian mansion to officially open as a bed-and-breakfast. I kept the mansion's original name, Pearl-by-the-Sea—affectionately referred to as the Pearl—and give it a new purpose. It had also given me a new purpose, and as proprietress, it was time to deal with my housekeeper problem.

I looked down at Greta, hoping my face was firm enough to grab her full attention. "It's important that everything is perfect by the time they arrive at ten o'clock."

Greta crossed her arms and frowned. "Who are these people, anyway?"

"I told you, the Vista County Genealogical and Historical Society."

She scrunched her face. "Piffle. I've got more history in my warts than that whole lot of them combined, let me tell you."

"You don't even know them. Would you please stop being a grouch and head back to the house to make sure everything is set up? I will be there to help as soon as I stop at the bakery." I held out my palm and raised an eyebrow, waiting.

Greta mumbled something, then fished the Vespa's keys from the folds in her puffy jacket and slapped them into my hand. "Suit yourself."

She turned away for the long trudge back to the house and I released a sigh of relief. Things didn't always go so easily with Greta. She was like an obstinate toddler most days, except smarter. And sneakier. Unpredictable.

I called after her, "Don't forget to prep the rooms. I want a fresh pitcher of water in every one. And fluff the pillows."

Greta didn't look back my way, but waved a dismissive hand in the air. "Yes, yes."

I frowned at her back. "And squirt some air freshener, too!"

***

I eased the scooter into an open parking space in front of the bakery. The mail truck parked outside told me Harper Tillman would be inside with Angie Owens, the baker. I stepped in, hoping a chat with friends would lighten my mood. Angie, at least, had a cheery disposition that rubbed off on even the orneriest of people, and she always had a kind word to share. She was the kindest, most generous person I knew.

"Absolutely not, Shelby." Angie shook her head with fists planted on her stout hips, face resolute. "You cannot use my baking trays. I can't believe you'd even suggest it."

"Oh, come on, dearie. I want to try out a new recipe and your sheets are better than my sheets."

Angie waved an empty tray in her hands. "These are top-of-the-line ceramic-coated, and I don't want you using them for experiments. They'll come back with margarine burns or heaven knows what."

Shelby bristled. "Margarine? I would never."

"Sorry," Angie said, setting the tray down softly. "That was cruel. I know you only use organic butter."

I crept to where Harper sat slumped against the wall at the bakery's single café table, her spindly legs outstretched in front of her. I slipped into the other seat. "Trouble?"

Harper rolled her heavy, lidded eyes. "I'll eat my mailbag if these two ever get their catering venture out of

6

the starting blocks."

Dressed in her usual uniform, Harper's tight brown ringlets lay tamed by a wide rainbow headband. A pair of bright socks peeked out from under the hem of her otherwise drab pants. She finished the outfit with a rainbow scarf looped around her long neck. As the local mail carrier—and the youngest to boot—Harper was well known around Starry Cove. I suppose in such a small town, everyone knew everyone else well enough, but the past few months taught me they only thought they did.

Our attention shifted back to the two women at the counter.

"I'm too busy to deal with this now. Can we talk about it later?" Angie's eyes flitted in our direction.

Shelby took the hint. "All right, dearie. I'll be next door at the diner using my own this time, but if my savory cheese puffs taste like twice-buried cardboard, you'll know whose fault it is."

Angie patted her hands on her floury apron and let out a heavy sigh as Shelby left. "Today has been insane, and it's barely started." She stretched high and pulled down two mugs from the upper cabinet. "Five birthday cake orders and a request for eight dozen peanut butter cookies." Grabbing the coffee pot off the large burner on the back counter, she filled the mugs and set them on the table between Harper and me. "All before eight o'clock." She returned with a mug of her own and plopped into the last seat at the table. Her short legs dangled a few inches above the floor and she tucked a loose brown curl behind an ear.

Harper's head leaned on the wall and nothing moved but her lips. "Rough morning, huh?"

"Are you still asleep?" Angie asked.

"You know I don't do mornings."

"It's nine o'clock already."

Harper grunted.

Angie pursed her lips. "Then what are you doing here?"

Harper sat up straighter. "Yeesh, Angie. What's gotten into you?"

"Sorry, sorry," Angie said, shaking her head and covering her face with both hands. "I don't know why I'm so snappy. It's just that the *Bake Shop Bliss* article comes out tomorrow and there are so many orders and Roy's out of town."

"Why's Roy gone?" I asked.

"My mother-in-law is ill, so he had to leave yesterday, and he'll be away for at least two weeks. Cesar's a great help here, but..." Angie frowned and studied her mug.

"Tomorrow will be great," I said. "Everyone will celebrate you. You'll be the toast of the town. Our very own celebrity."

"Oh, stop," Angie said, waving me off, but a rosiness bloomed in her cheeks. "What about you? First guests, that's exciting."

"If only Greta would behave."

"What now?" Harper asked.

I shook my head. "She commandeered the Vespa again."

"I thought I heard it go by earlier while I was rolling out cookies. Like a dying goat bleating to be put out of its misery."

"Sounds about right." Harper gave me a stern look.

"Still want to keep her?"

My shoulders dropped. "I need her help at the house. There's always so much to do. And she does a lot—all the cooking, especially."

In my past life, I ran a hotel with my now-ex-husband, but there had been staff to keep it all running smoothly. When I decided to renovate my late uncle Arthur's house and turn it into a bed-and-breakfast, I suppose I thought I'd be able to do it all myself. Turns out, I was a terrible cook and not so good at keeping up with all the work. Greta, on the other hand, had a gourmet touch and a reliable work ethic, but only when she could stay focused. When she showed up at the house unexpectedly looking for her old friend Arthur, I didn't have the heart to turn her away and she just sort of stuck. Like an old wad of gum, she stuck.

Angie nodded knowingly. "It feels like a mountain of tasks that will never get done."

"Yeah. Especially now that I have official guests."

Harper took a swig of coffee. "Okay, whatever, if you insist on having her around. I know I don't have to remind you of the time she drugged a bunch of people at your house. Or when she ripped all the upholstery off your antique furniture. Or the time—"

"I know, I know."

Harper sneered. "Who is she, anyway? Does she even have a last name, or does she fancy herself another Cher or Madonna? It's so weird. It's like you've adopted this stray old lady and keep her around like a pet."

"She's… I don't know." I shook my head. "I guess she is like family. So she's staying, okay?"

Harper pinched her face. "Suit yourself," she said in

a nasally voice, mocking Greta's signature phrase.

"Well, I think it's sweet."

"Thank you, Angie. I know the situation with Greta is unconventional, but it works. Usually."

Angie lowered her voice. "Has she found anything about the map?"

Oh, yeah, the map. She meant the map we found under the upholstery of the aforementioned ripped antique furniture. "No, but she's in the library at the house every day, reading through what must be the driest, most mind-numbing subjects ever. Honestly, you'd think Arthur was the dullest person if his book collection is any sign."

"It's just a matter of time," Angie said. "She's found useful information in there before."

Harper nearly choked, sputtering, and wiped coffee off her chin with her scarf. "Useful?"

"You know what I mean."

"If you call sending us into a pit in the earth in the middle of the forest to discover nothing but a looted, booby-trapped burial chamber useful, then I suppose so."

I rested my face in my hand and blew a strand of black hair out of my eyes. "She's such a Luddite, though. She refuses to search the internet or use anything electronic. I'm surprised she's so interested in the scooter."

Harper whipped out her phone, checking the time. "How the heck did she and Arthur do any research without the *internet*?"

Angie chortled. "Some of us remember the days when there was no internet."

"I even got her a card for the Vista County Library. I was going to give it to her today, but she's on my naughty list."

Angie seemed doubtful. "Will she even use it?"

My eye twinkled and a smug grin spread across my face. "I have an incentive."

Before I could explain, Cesar, Angie's bakery assistant, swung through the doors from the back kitchen, hauling a massive tray of cinnamon rolls fresh from the oven. He wore an apron, like Angie, but unlike Angie he was tall, with thick dark hair and strong arms.

Our chatter stopped cold, and he stutter-stepped when he spotted the three of us staring at him.

"Hi there, Poppy," he said. "You look nice today."

I peered down at my pink denim overalls and muddy sneakers. The oversized gray cardigan I grabbed as I left the mansion this morning drooped over my shoulders.

"Thanks," I said, a little confused.

A faint smile touched Angie's lips, but she said nothing.

Harper was less tactful. "Hello to you, too, Cesar. You're looking awfully floury today."

He stepped behind the counter and set the tray down. "Oh, hi Harper."

She rolled her eyes my way, peering at me from the side, and I shrugged. He finished loading the rolls onto a display tray on the counter and disappeared back into the kitchen with a quick wave.

Angie and Harper turned sharply in my direction.

"What?" I asked. "He's just being nice. Clearly, he thought I needed a compliment."

"Uh huh." Angie tried to hold back her grin.

"Hey, how's Ryan doing?"

"Harper," Angie admonished, "be quiet."

"It's okay," I said. "I have to pick something up at

the general store later today, so I'll probably see him there." I smiled weakly, but I was dreading it. Ryan—Dr. MacKenzie—would likely be at the pharmacy's tiny nook inside the store. Just the thought of seeing him made my stomach flutter and churn at the same time.

Angie laid a hand on mine. "Have you two even talked recently?"

I shook my head. "Only a few passing words here and there. It's like he's avoiding me."

Harper finished her coffee with a final gulp. "This is why I don't bother with men."

"I'm sure he has a reason to be so distant. When Roy and I started dating, he stopped talking to me for a whole month. I only found out later it was because he chipped a tooth and didn't want to show me his hideous smile until he could get it fixed. It was actually really romantic."

"It's gotta be something, though," Harper said. "It's not like you grew three heads overnight."

I checked the time. "Greta should be back at the house by now, and I'll want to do a walkthrough before any of these genealogy folks arrive. Were those the cinnamon rolls I ordered that Cesar brought out?"

Angie hopped off the chair. "I have them all set. I just need to wrap them up." She slipped behind the counter and unfurled a long swath of cling film. "I'm so excited about the presentation they're doing for our little town."

Harper grunted.

"What presentation?" I asked.

Angie dropped her arms and stared at me in dismay. "Don't you remember? The ancestry reading they're doing for the townspeople who submitted requests last month. That's the whole reason they booked the Pearl."

"Oh," I said, rubbing my temple. "It must have slipped my mind."

"Did you submit a request, or did that slip your mind as well?"

"No, no, I did."

"Good," Angie said, tipping her head and smiling in a satisfied manner. A heavy tray appeared in her arms from under the counter. "It'll be fun to find out all the interesting things about our families, won't it?"

Harper grunted again.

"I've found out enough interesting tidbits about Arthur to last a lifetime."

"Besides Arthur, then."

"Maybe," I said, doubtful.

"Maybe…" Harper began and sat up, finally joining the conversation. "Maybe Lily isn't your real sister. Wouldn't that be a shock?"

"Not likely," Angie said. "They look almost iden—"

"Shoot," I said, slapping my hand on my knee. "I was supposed to call her back."

"Who, Lily? How is she doing?" Angie's voice was full of concern. "Are the cancer treatments working?"

"They're working, last I heard, and she's as *pleasant* as usual. She left me a message yesterday asking me to call her back, but I forgot. I'll have to do it later, though." I got up from my chair and hefted the tray of cinnamon rolls from Angie's arms. "I need to get to the house before anyone arrives. Wouldn't be good to have Greta as my first impression."

Angie and Harper exchanged cringing glances as I stepped out the door.

Two

A SHORT WALK from the bakery brought me to the Pearl, situated at the entrance to town. A big purple thing, it loomed over the landscape like a watchtower and greeted visitors who turned off the nearby highway looking for a hideaway village to while away a few hours.

The color was all Arthur—it was an eye-catching purple from the moment I drove up nearly a year ago to take over the property. I curved along the sidewalk that made the roundabout at the town entrance, a circular road with a flagpole at its center, and Main Street jutted out in one direction, ending at the beach.

A commotion and jostling bodies came into view on the wrap-around porch and a man's brash voice carried to me on the sidewalk. "Now listen here, whoever you are, we're guests at this establishment. We've paid to stay here, and I expect to be accommodated."

"What's going on?" I asked as I hurried under a white trellis and along the walkway leading up from the road.

A tall man in an expensive looking trench coat and

wool cap, holding two bags, one in either hand, turned and eyed me up and down with a pair of piercing blue eyes. "Who are you?" he demanded.

I finished my last stride to the porch and stopped next to this man. A younger woman with a short brown bob and thin-rimmed glasses waited behind him. She favored her left arm, which hung useless in a sling. To my great displeasure, Greta stood like a boulder in the doorway, hands on her hips.

"I'm Poppy Lewis," I said firmly. "I own this place. How may I assist you?"

"This woman," he said, sneering at Greta, "refuses to let us into the building. She says we cannot come in until our reservation."

Greta grunted and didn't budge. "They aren't due until ten o'clock. I don't even have the tea brewing yet."

"My taxi has already driven off. What am I supposed to do with these?" He held up a leather overnight bag and motioned with his head toward what appeared to be a filing box tucked under his arm.

"Mine's just left, too," the meek woman said. Her voice was so soft I nearly missed that she'd said anything at all.

"I'm sorry for the confusion." I leveled an exasperated look at Greta, who pursed her lips defiantly, then maneuvered my way past the grouchy man and shifted the tray of cinnamon rolls to one hand and opened the front door with the other. Standing aside and nudging Greta out of the way with my hip, I welcomed them over the threshold and into the foyer.

"Finally." The man, tall and bulky, shoved his way in first, past the timid woman, leaving her to manage her own luggage. Weighed down by two bags dangling on her one working arm, she stepped into the house in an ungainly fashion and let her suitcases drop to the floor.

With a flick of my head, I motioned to Greta to carry the rest of the young woman's bags inside.

"But it's not ten o'clock," Greta growled. "You said ten o'clock."

Forcing down my exasperation, I whispered through a smile, "Have some common sense, would you?"

Greta grumbled again, but complied, and once inside, I could finally greet my first guests in the foyer of my renovated bed-and-breakfast. "Welcome," I said, "to the Pearl-by-the-Sea. We hope you enjoy your stay."

My eyes flicked to Greta, whose wrinkled face stared straight ahead at nothing before spotting me. She gave a sudden start. "Oh, uh, likewise," she said flatly and set down the luggage.

"What a beautiful house," the woman said, turning to me. "I'm Ivy Bridger. This is—"

The man shoved a hand forward. "Randall Portsmouth, CG, CGP, FSP."

I shook his hand firmly and looked straight into his eyes, ensuring he didn't mistake me for a person he could steamroll like he did Ivy. "Poppy Lewis, as I mentioned before. And this is Greta—just Greta—the housekeeper and cook. I'm sure you'll love what she has to offer."

Randall turned up his nose. "If it's anything like what we've already been offered, I'll pass, thank you very much."

"I'm sure it will be lovely," Ivy said, nodding at Greta.

Greta's emotionless face transformed into a beaming

smile. She rocked back on her heels, and opened her mouth to say something, but I cut her off. "Yes, yes. I'm sure of it." It was never a good idea to let Greta talk too much. I'd had previous complaints regarding her uncouth topics of conversation and proposals that would make a roughneck blink twice. Best to avoid those scenarios again, if possible.

I quickly handed Greta the cinnamon rolls and turned back to my guests. "Why don't I show you up to your rooms while we wait for everyone else to arrive? Here," I said, picking up Ivy's bags in both hands, "I'll get these and we can head upstairs."

Randall let his eyes wander from the foyer to the main living space and back to the stairwell leading up-stairs. "The building isn't as spectacular in person as I thought it might be. And the purple is even more garish than the pictures led me to believe."

"I like the purple," Ivy said.

Randall let out a hefty sigh and shook his head. "Of course you would like it."

Ivy dropped her eyes as we climbed to the second floor, where doors to four large rooms led off from the landing.

"There is a washroom here." I gestured to a closed door next to the head of the stairwell. "The door sticks sometimes."

With my arms full of Ivy's luggage, I led her to her room first. Each room accommodated two guests—separate beds, of course—and she'd be sharing with another woman who had yet to arrive. After hefting a bag's handle onto my forearm, I tugged at the doorknob with my free hand and entered the room.

"Oh, how wonderful," Ivy said and twirled as she entered the brightly lit room. She quickly caught herself and stopped, abashed, and looked away.

Even with the foggy gloom bearing down outside, the large windows let in a surprising amount of light, especially in the morning hours. I silently thanked Greta for opening the drapes, otherwise, we would have walked into a dark and drab space, although I was pretty sure Ivy's reaction would have been just as positive.

"It's not much, but each room keeps its original charm, even after the recent renovations. I made sure of that."

Randall dipped his head in from the landing and peered around, taking stock. "Adequate. Quite adequate."

I took that as a compliment. "Thanks. Ivy, I've set your bags here on the bed. Why don't you make yourself comfortable? Make your way downstairs as you'd like while I show Randall to his room."

Ivy's short hair glowed in the light from the window. "Thank you," she said quickly before turning back to gaze outward. The window faced east, toward the roundabout, and still caught the morning's waning light.

I'd climbed out of that window one night. A rainy night not too long past, but I pushed the memory down and returned to the landing. Randall waited, tapping his leather-tooled shoes, and muttered something under his breath when I appeared.

"This way," I said, guiding him toward the most elegant room in the entire mansion—the Victorian Suite. The group doubled-up when they found out I only had four rooms to reserve, although each could accommodate two boarders comfortably and separately. The Victorian

Suite, however, housed the antique furniture left to me by Arthur, and its grand elegance was the pride of the Pearl. I'd chosen this room for Randall and his roommate because the roommate—not Randall—was the head of the genealogical society and the grand Victorian bed was reserved for his use.

I glided into the room and heard Randall's exhale of surprise behind me. It was as expected, and a slight grin touched my lips, which he could not see. I composed myself and turned around with a smile. "Lovely, isn't it?"

"It's magnificent," he said, taking in the elaborately carved and upholstered furniture which graced the large room. Glints of golden gilding gleamed from every corner.

Stepping toward the back of the room, I pushed aside the screen that separated the large Victorian bed and the smaller, less ornate single bed prepared for Randall. The second frame of the screen caught on its own old, rusty hinge, refusing to bend, so I bent down to unsnag it. With a grunt I pulled it free and straightened, saying to Randall, "I hope these accommodations—" but I stopped as I noticed Randall unpacking a few books from the leather bag he'd placed squarely on the duvet of the Victorian bed.

"This will do nicely." He pushed on the bed in quick succession, testing the firmness of the mattress. "Yes, quite nicely."

"Oh, I…" My words faded as I looked doubtfully at the smaller bed tucked behind the screen, then back at Randall, whose nose seemed to point upward at just the right angle to make you feel small. Sighing, I pulled the screen closed. "Excellent," I said, circling back to Randall. "Please join me downstairs when you've settled in for beverages and morning snacks."

"I'm not one to *snack*." He said the word as though coated in oil. "But I will be down shortly. No doubt the others will arrive soon."

This reminder sent me scurrying back down the stairs with a hasty farewell. Greta and fresh, unsuspecting guests would not be a good combination.

My timing was excellent, as the doorbell rang just as I took the last stair into the foyer. Greta appeared around the corner from the kitchen, but I held up my hand and she retreated. A mix of elevated voices, not in anger or agitation, but in excitement, greeted me as I swung open the front door.

Two sturdy women of middle age and an elderly gentleman bundled in a cozy green sweater turned and greeted me warmly. "Hello there," the man said with a smile. "You must be Poppy Lewis."

I recognized his voice as Julian Gaines, the leader of the ancestry group, with whom I'd shared numerous phone calls while scheduling the group's stay. He had a warm smile, with straight white teeth, and his close-cropped brown curls were more gray than brown. It was nice to finally put a face to his voice. "Come in," I said, gesturing for the throng to enter. "Come in, please."

The women returned to their chatter as they bustled into the foyer. Greta appeared again, but remained in the entryway to the kitchen. This was the routine we'd discussed and rehearsed. I would greet the guests and she would appear for introductions.

As I closed the door, a hefty orange tomcat hurried in from the cold air outside and took up a spot on the first stair.

"That fellow must belong to you," said Julian, nodding toward the cat.

"Mayor Dewey?" I let out a chuckle. "No, he's not mine. He's the town mayor."

"Your mayor?" one of the middle-aged women asked. She flipped her spectacles down from the top of her head where they'd perched like a headband to get a better look at Dewey, who lazed on the stairs, washing a paw.

"That's right," Julian said, nodding. "You mentioned that on the phone." He turned to the two women. "It was in the *Vista View* a while back."

"Oh yes, I remember that now," she replied. Her hair was cut short and salt-and-pepper throughout, and after a sufficient observation of Mayor Dewey, she returned her glasses onto her head as they were before. "How charming."

I stepped forward and held out a hand to the salt-and-pepper woman. "Nice to meet you, I'm Poppy. Welcome to the Pearl-by-the-Sea."

She took my hand, not in a shake, but in a gentle embrace, and greeted me with a kind smile. "Yeardley Mitchell."

The other woman stepped in and held out her own hand. "Candace Filby. Thanks for having us." Hers was a firm handshake, which matched her demeanor. She was a sturdy woman, tall and confident, with full, shoulder-length hair dyed a bold copper. The slight wrinkles around her eyes were the only thing that gave away her age.

"Two others have already arrived," I said. "Ivy and Randall. They should be down shortly." At the mention of Randall's name, Yeardley's kind face disclosed a hint of displeasure, and Candace openly scowled. Julian did not seem to react at all, except to thank me once again for the hospitality.

A gruff clearing of a throat sounded from behind where I stood, and I realized I'd forgotten to introduce Greta. I stepped aside so the newly arrived guests could see her. "My housekeeper and cook, Greta." Greta stood a little taller and grinned proudly, wires of course gray hair poked out from the loose braid she'd cobbled together after her clandestine scooter ride. "She's an absolute wonder and work-horse in the kitchen." Her grin spread even wider. "That's why we'll see very little of her, unfortunately." Her grin disappeared, and she glowered at me, but I was already ushering the three guests upstairs to their rooms.

"The house is so striking." Candace's colorful hair whipped around as she took it all in.

Yeardley nodded. "Definitely built to impress."

"It was my uncle's," I said, "but I think he moved in during the sixties or seventies, so it's seen a few different owners."

"Not a family estate?" Julian asked me, confused.

"No, although he passed it down to me in his will. He had no children of his own."

A trio of nods and mm-hmms followed as I led them to their rooms. Yeardley and Candace would share one of the remaining suites, and Julian would be with Randall, although bunking on the smaller bed since Randall had claimed the stately Victorian. He did not seem to mind, however, and thanked me once again as I retreated downstairs to let them settle in.

Ivy and Randall must have made their way to the living room while I was occupied in a room upstairs, because when I took the final step, Randall's haughty drawl floated in from the living room.

"I'm not saying you're wrong, Ivy. I'm just exploring the idea that your sources may be of questionable origin. As you may know, while researching my fourth collection—"

The doorbell chime cut him off. "That must be the others," I said quickly, hoping to escape what was sure to be an extended monologue by Randall.

"No doubt," he replied with a sniff. "I believe I heard the beastly sputtering of William's motorbike a moment ago."

There were three guests yet to arrive, and two more, both men, waited on the porch as I opened the door. I stared for a moment, as both men could not be more different from one another. The first, portly, aging, and bearded, stood with his thumbs hooked in the loops of his dirty blue jeans. A grease-stained white shirt was all he wore under an oversized black leather jacket with a logo of a wolf riding a motorcycle on the left front chest. The words "Lone Riders" was emblazoned underneath. Heavy boots finished out the look, and he carried nothing but a beat-up and ratty duffel bag. The other man stood formal and rigid, with his black hair slicked back at graying temples. He wore a meticulously tailored blue suit and carried a single case of fine luggage. They made an odd couple.

"Poppy Lewis?" the slick man ventured.

I shook off my surprise. "Yes. Please come in both of you."

The dapper man shook my hand. "Everett Ayers."

The other followed him in with a quick nod of his head in my direction. "William Boyd," he said in a deep baritone.

Greta slumped out from the kitchen, the pep gone from earlier, and I introduced her to the new arrivals. Before she could retreat, I caught her arm. "This would be a good time to set out refreshments."

"The usual?"

"Yes, but don't forget the cinnamon rolls."

She grunted and slumped back into the kitchen.

By now, the other guests had made their way down and mingled in the large living room with Randall and Ivy. I led William and Everett up to their shared room. Julian made it clear on the phone that Randall and William were not to be placed together, and offered to room with Randall outright to avoid any drama.

As with the others, I let Everett and William get situated and pointed out the relevant landmarks such as the washroom and their individual spaces within the large shared room. William pitched his duffel onto one of the two beds and waited patiently for me by the door. Everett lingered, unpacking suits from his garment bag and placing them with care into the stately armoire against the far wall.

"I'll leave you to it," I said to Everett. "Let me know if you need anything, otherwise, you can join us downstairs whenever you'd like."

William followed closely as I descended to the living room. It was good to hear the energetic sounds of lively conversation, as it made my job as host much easier. The group all stood in a tight circle, deep in a discussion about what sounded like the questionable parentage of Lord Something-or-other.

"Don't be obtuse," Randall said as I walked up. "The patrilineage of the second son was never definitively proven, but if we examine—"

"Has everyone settled in all right?" This was met with gracious nods or thankful smiles from all but Randall. Candace placed a hand on Yeardley's arm as if to say she'd be right back, and stepped away, joining me on the fringe of the bustling group.

She let out a hearty chuckle, and her hair swung like a sheet of coppery rain with each guffaw. "You'll be bored to tears and sick of us by the end of the week, Poppy. I guarantee it."

"Oh no," I protested. "I'm sure it's fascinating."

"You'd never guess there'd be so much controversy over the parentage of some man who lived hundreds of years ago, but then again," she lowered her voice, "it's not uncommon for the vegetable to come from a neighbor's patch, if you get my meaning." She nudged me with her elbow.

"I'm sure," I replied with an acquiescent smile. "Greta may need my help in the kitchen. Would you please excuse me?"

"Of course, of course." Candace patted me on the shoulder and then returned to the fray, jumping back into the conversation at hand. "You forgot about the entry in the town Bible, which clearly showed…"

Her voice faded as I swung into the kitchen. Greta humming to herself and waving her hips with the tune, finished setting the final cinnamon roll on a decorative glass tray. She'd even put down doilies first. Despite her unruly appearance, she had a knack for all things cooking. Her dishes were not only delicious and imaginative, but they were displayed beautifully. Utterly irresistible.

"Just finished," she said, stepping off the tiny wooden stool she used to reach the counter. "Tea and coffee are ready, too." She wiped her hands on her apron, and after a moment whispered, "The kettle was whistling something to me—couldn't quite make it out—so maybe don't drink the tea."

"I'm sure it's fine," I said and grabbed the nearby tray of mugs and teacups. Her cooking was amazing, but her quirks were abundant and often unsettling. They were generally harmless, and I'd learned to roll with them and hoped they didn't manifest in front of guests too frequently. "Let's get these set out."

In a rehearsed dance, we spun through the swing door from the kitchen to the adjacent dining space, which included a large table and sideboard, where I quickly set down my tray, and Greta followed suit with the cinnamon rolls. I returned to the kitchen and picked up the large carafe of hot coffee just as the doorbell rang again. The final guest had arrived.

I twirled through the doorway once again, eager to set down the coffee, Candace called out from the adjoining common room. "I've got it, Poppy. You carry on."

With my arms laden with scalding liquid, I was thankful for the extra hand and only slightly embarrassed that one guest had to get the door for another. Greta and I took a few minutes setting out the carafes, mugs, napkins, and other bits and bobs before I could rejoin the others in the common room.

Everett had appeared within the group, and was

already deep in conversation with Julian. "Where's Candace?" I asked, noticing she was missing.

Yeardley was the first to answer. "She's already upstairs helping Olivia with her bags." I moved toward the stairwell in the foyer to join them, not wanting to leave my guests to fend for themselves, but Yeardley added, "Don't worry, they're fine."

"But she won't know the way."

"There's only one spot left." Yeardley tsked and shook her head. "Olivia's always the last to arrive at our meetings, too."

"She lacks in punctuality," said Randall. "Not a trait normally associated with those who take their participation in this society seriously."

William crossed his arms and responded, "Why don't you get off your high horse just for once, Randall, and spare the rest of us."

Randall bristled. "I'll have you know—"

"Tea anyone?" I broke in. "We've set out refreshments in the dining room, including fresh cinnamon rolls from our local bakery."

"I won't say no to cinnamon rolls," Yeardley said, her eyes lighting up.

"Yes, thank you," Julian said with an exasperated sigh. "This would be a good time for refreshments."

"We have tea, coffee, and of course, water. What can I get for everyone?"

"Nothing for me." Randall waved a dismissive hand.

"I'm sure Yeardley wants coffee," said Julian. "She drinks it like a fish."

"Correct," she replied. "The hotter and steamier, the better. The perfect cup of coffee makes my glasses steam up in just the right way."

"All right," I said. "One coffee."

William raised a hand. "Make that two. And I don't care how steamy it is."

"Tea for me, please," said Julian.

Everett's voice was calm. "I will also have tea."

"Just water for me," Ivy whispered before adding a timid "thank you" on the end.

Suggesting they all get comfortable, I headed to the dining room, and set about preparing their drinks. I returned and made my way around, serving their beverage of choice and offered a cinnamon roll to each.

William took his mug of coffee just as his phone rang. When he pulled it from his pocket, he sighed. "It's the gang again. I've gotta take this one." He lumbered out of the deep, cushioned chair and made his way to the porch.

Randall, who sat opposite, laughed scornfully after he'd left. "'The gang,' indeed. If he's part of a motorcycle gang, then I'm Genghis Khan's grandson."

Yeardley thanked me as she took her coffee and cinnamon roll off the tray, then peered around me to address Randall. "You may actually be, you know. At least partly."

"Don't you go babbling on about everyone being Genghis Khan's descendants. It's nothing but an old wives' tale. Honestly, I'd expect better from this group than latching on to every fanciful story you read in the dredges of your so-called research." Randall huffed and stood up from the seat he'd just taken. "I'm going upstairs to work on my manuscript. Or to rest, since you're all giving me an atrocious headache." He grabbed two cinnamon rolls off the tray I held, mumbling something about immersing one's self in the local culinary culture, and retreated to the stairs. On his way, Randall passed Candace and Olivia.

"Who put a bee in his bonnet?" Candace asked after she reached the group.

"Just Randall being Randall." Julian sounded tired. He sat deeply in a large high-backed chair near a panel window of ornate stained glass flanking the fireplace—one of the home's original features.

"As long as he keeps his moods to himself," Candace replied.

I greeted Olivia, whom I hadn't met before. "I'm sorry I wasn't able to see you to your room. I hope you got settled all right?"

"Yes, fine. Thanks." Her voice was confident. Younger than Yeardley and Candace, and older than Ivy, I thought she may have been in her early thirties at the most. She wore her honey hair in a sensible pony tail, letting the long waves fall haphazardly down her back and was dressed in comfortable clothing—jeans and a simple gray sweater. If her hair were black and she were a few years older, she would have reminded me of myself.

Her attention shifted to the group. "Wasting no time getting into the meat of it, I see."

"You know us so well," Yeardley said with a wink. She smiled up at me. "I hope you're taking part in our little reveal tomorrow, Poppy."

"Yes, I've put my name in, and I know others are looking forward to it as well."

Olivia plopped down in the chair vacated by Randall. "I heard there's a Scottish guy in town. Did anyone get him?"

My ears perked up at this comment. They must mean Ryan.

"He's mine," said Candace with a sly grin.

"Dr. Makenzie," I said with more excitement in my voice than I meant to utter. "He's our pharmacist."

Candace nodded knowingly. "I'll be reporting on him at the event tomorrow."

"Anything interesting?" Olivia asked.

"Maybe." Candace's eyes flicked my way. "I shouldn't say anything, though. Let it be a surprise." The faint smile didn't leave her face, and she held my gaze a moment longer.

My shoulders slumped. Of course Ryan would be interesting. Despite his sensible V-neck sweater and wrinkled lab coat, I was drawn to him, which made the recent diversion of our budding relationship even more frustrating. I had to repair what was broken. It gnawed at me, and I'd let it go on too long. For now, I tended to my guests, but the general store was the next thing on my agenda and he was sure to be there. It was time to finally find out why he'd been avoiding me.

Three

WITH THE GUESTS properly settled, refreshed, and stuffed with cinnamon rolls, I headed to the general store, safe in the knowledge that they were so engrossed in their discussion about the maternal line of Dorothea Duckworth, first female mayor of Vista, that they wouldn't notice my departure. I now faced the dreaded doors to the store, wrapped in a heavy scarf, my breath puffing into little clouds and drifted away on the chilly mid-day air. Inside, I would find Ursula, the shopkeeper, shuffling about and stocking her wares, but I would also find our good doctor, Ryan MacKenzie. It was time to face the music, as they say, so I steeled myself and stepped inside.

And there he was—brown hair cut short, but not too short. Rimless eyeglasses perched on his nose—a nose that was neither too small nor too large. Today's V-neck sweater was pale blue to match his eyes, and his lab coat was wrinkled in the most endearing way. Ryan, whom I'd sworn was only a friend for so long, but whose absence over the past few months seemed to make my heart grow fonder. Angie understood, but Harper had just rolled her eyes and said I was silly for not going for it full-steam. But fresh off a divorce, I'd been reluctant to move faster than a snail's pace, even if the perfect man stood right in front of me.

Ryan and Ursula, her hair dyed a shocking shade of red today, chatted near the main counter, and it was she who spotted me first. "Hello there, Poppy," she called out.

At the mention of my name, Ryan glanced my way. I smiled weakly, and thankfully, he smiled back. But there was little excitement in it, more like an anxious or nervous tick than genuine affection. What had changed between us?

I joined them and asked Ursula, "Has my order come in yet?"

"Sorry, Poppy," she said. "There was some kind of shipping delay. I'll be sure to let you know when they're here. Or Ryan can—I know he always shares what's new in stock."

Used to share, she meant. Before he started avoiding me.

"Maybe I'll just come back in a few days," I said. "It's hardly a long walk from the Pearl, anyway."

"Oh, yes, your grand opening." Ursula said. "How's that going? Ryan and I were just talking about the upcoming meeting, weren't we?"

"Er, yes," he said in his annoying and perfectly impish Scottish accent. "Should be quite a show."

"Did you put your name in, Poppy? For the ancestry review, I mean."

"I did."

"Us too," Ursula said, eyes lighting up. "I'm so

excited to find out what secrets lurk in my family's history."

"I'd be careful what you wish for," Ryan said with a chuckle. "Don't know what salacious details might come out that you can't squeeze back in the bottle."

Ursula waved him off. "I'm up for any surprises. I don't shame easily, you know—have you seen my hair today? I asked for mahogany and I got circus red. That's the last time I go to a hairdresser recommended by Shelby, let me tell you."

"It is a tad bright," Ryan admitted.

"I'm sure it will fade to a nice mahogany. Or crimson, at least."

"It'll be purple next week, anyway. I like to keep it fresh—just not circus-fresh. Anyway," she said, patting my arm, "tell us about your guests. Have they told you anything about us or who our famous ancestors are? Am I related to a celebrity?"

I shook my head. "Nothing like that, I'm afraid. Although, we might all be descendants of Genghis Khan."

Ursula blinked. "Genghis who?"

Ryan let a small smile touch his lips, and I couldn't help but smile, too.

"Just one of the greatest conquerors of all time," he said.

Ursula seemed unimpressed. "Well, if he's not on the television or in the magazines, I doubt I'd care. Now, if we were all related to Burt Reynolds, that's something to get excited about."

"I'd say so," I said, "since we'd all be cousins, even the married ones."

"There's that." She frowned. "Guess we'll find out

tomorrow. I've got to get back to stocking these shelves. You two carry on."

Before I could catch her arm, Ursula had tottered off down the personal hygiene aisle, leaving Ryan and I standing alone.

He teetered back and forth on his heels, staring at the ground. I guess this was it.

"How have you been?" I asked with an awkward level of pep in my voice, hoping the question sounded light and insignificant rather than holding the weight of our entire future together.

"Oh, you know. Busy. Very busy."

"Busy," I repeated, nodding. It took me another moment to muster the courage to add, "I haven't seen you in a while. Is everything okay?"

"Me?" The shock in his voice sounded stiff and artificial.

"How's the gazebo project going?" This was a poor attempt at making conversation, and I kicked myself inside as soon as I asked. Ryan had been trying to build a gazebo in his backyard for months, continually thwarted by a string of unreliable builders and his own poor carpentry skills.

"Still in shambles, I'm afraid."

We stood in awkward silence for a few moments after that. I'd come here for a reason, though, and I girded myself before taking a deep breath. "Have you..." I bit my lip. "Have you been avoiding me?"

He didn't answer straight away, and he still stared at the ground. It was so unlike him, the man I knew who, although reserved, was still forthright and candid. "I just, ah, didn't know how to approach things."

"Things?"

"You and, ah, that actor fellow."

Actor fellow? I wracked my brains, but came up at a loss. Finally, I had to ask. "What actor fellow?"

He tucked his hands in the pockets of his lab coat, then took them back out and crossed his arms before uncrossing and shoving them back in his pockets. "That superstar fellow."

My mouth worked silently, repeating his words, trying to understand who he meant. I worked backward in time, remembering the moments of purposeful avoidance, the cold shoulders, the missed opportunities, until I landed on the answer—Devin Evers. He must mean the theater actor and very, very not-my-type Devin Evers. It was such a surprising—and absurd—revelation, that I hardly knew how to respond, so the words tumbled out of my mouth, twinged with incredulity, "From the broken-down theater bus a few months ago?"

He squirmed in place and didn't meet my eyes.

"The man who refused to eat carbohydrates?"

"You seemed cozy enough to have breakfast with him. In *our* booth, mind you." He sounded irritated—or whatever level of irritation Ryan could show—as if his entire argument wasn't the most illogical thing I'd ever heard.

My initial surprised now turned to frustration. If I was hearing Ryan correctly, he'd been avoiding me because he was jealous that I'd had breakfast at the diner with a beautiful man who had no romantic interest in me and in whom I had less-than-zero romantic interest. "Are you kidding me?"

His eyes widened behind his glasses—I hadn't held

back with my tone.

"Are you kidding me?" I repeated. "All this time you've shrugged me off because I ate breakfast in the vicinity of another man? Who, I will remind you again, is absolutely not my type and probably has no interest in me, either."

I may have blurted out the last part a bit loudly, as Ursula turned from her work to look at us.

Ryan lowered his own voice to a near-whisper. "It's more than that, to be honest."

Oh no, here it was—the truth. Regardless of my admonishment, I wasn't prepared for something worse. I steeled myself.

"It's my son," he said.

The tension left my body. "Your son?"

"Aye. Ethan's had a rough go of it the past few months, acting out a wee bit, that sort of thing. Pappo and Mommo—those are his grandparents—can't reign him in. And they shouldn't have to. He's my child, my responsibility."

My anger and frustration faded. Ryan's concern for his son was clear. Despite a previous marriage, I had no children of my own. My focus had been on my business, and with my ex-husband, it never seemed like the right time.

"So, he's coming to live with me," he continued. "Vista isn't that far of a drive, so he'll still attend school there, and Pappo and Mommo will still help where they can, but he'll live with me full time, here in Starry Cove."

I opened my mouth to speak, but Ryan held up a hand and went on. "And it's a difficult time for distractions, Poppy. I hope you know what I mean. For my son's sake, at least."

I dropped my eyes. "I understand."

"It's not that I've been avoiding you, but I need to sort things out with Ethan."

"Right."

"I hope you aren't too angry with me. I just need to go slow."

"Slow." I nodded as I repeated the word, but inside I was a ball of confusion. If things moved any slower with Ryan we'd be overtaken by a sloth. I hadn't even kissed the man!

"Thanks," he said, patting me on the shoulder like an old friend. "I knew you'd understand." He smiled weakly as he returned to the pharmacy alcove in the back, leaving me standing and staring at nothing in the middle of the store.

"Everything all right, Poppy?"

I shook myself out of my daze and turned to find Ursula by my side.

"Yes, fine," I said.

Ursula looked toward Ryan, then back to me. "His son's been giving him a real hard time. Must be tough for him—takes all of his focus, if you know what I mean."

I said nothing, but bit my lip and let her continue.

"My son used to give me grief, too. I finally found him a hobby that kept him busy and out of trouble." She nodded sagely. "He grew out of his problems and now he's a fine young man, if I do say so myself. A fine young man."

"I'm sure he is," I said. "But I should get back to my guests before they burn the place down." I smiled, forcing a light-hearted chuckle, and headed for the door.

***

A cacophony of voices greeted me as I stepped inside the mansion. More discussion about grandparents and marriages and fourth cousins twice removed. I hadn't been gone long enough for them to notice, and Candace waved me over as I entered the room.

"What's your take on marriages between cousins?" she asked me with a hearty laugh. "William seems to think the line should be drawn at second cousins, while Olivia swears you have to go four generations back in order for it to be kosher."

"I don't really—"

"I said third cousins," William corrected her, cutting me off. "Stop trying to make me sound like some hill-billy."

"You do a perfectly fine job of doing that yourself," Olivia said and took a casual sip of water from a dainty glass, eyeing William over the rim.

Candace spit out her coffee in a burst of laughter and immediately blotted it up with her napkin. "Sorry Poppy. We're an absolute mess when we're allowed to congregate together."

"It's all right," I said. "I'd better check on Greta."

"She's in the little room off the entryway." Candace pointed toward the library. "Scurried in there quick-as-you-like and shut the door after someone asked her for a phone charger. Haven't seen her since."

I thanked Candace with a grimace and entered the library. Greta sat cross-legged on a puffy chair in one corner, her nose buried deep in a leather-bound book.

"It's not time to start dinner yet," she said without

looking up.

"I know. How did everything go while I was gone?"

"Fine. People mingled."

"Uh-huh." I crossed my arms. "And you hid in—"

"I'm not hiding."

"You're hiding because of a phone charger."

Greta stared into her book.

"You've got to get over your fear of electronics," I said finally, exasperated.

"A healthy skepticism is not fear."

"A phone charger will not steal your brainwaves."

She snapped the book shut. "And since when are you the scientific expert?"

I closed my eyes and inhaled deeply, remembering the particular techniques I'd practiced to keep me from losing my cool. I counted backward in my head. Three, two, one. "All right, Greta," I said calmly. "I'll leave you to your *studies*. I just hope all the time you've spent locked away in here comes to some fruition."

She eyed me sideways. "I'm still looking."

I gave a curt nod, and as I turned to leave, a heavy thumping sounded on the staircase above my head. "What the…"

Entering the foyer, Randall, pale and disheveled, stumbled down the last few stairs, his mouth working silently as each foot landed unsteadily. In his daze, he failed to maneuver the last steps, and fell into my arms. His slick, sweaty hands pawed at my sweater, and his drooping blue eyes, like pools of water, stared into mine without seeing. I shrieked as his weight pulled me down.

The others rushed over at my cries, then backed away when Randall lurched from atop of me and dragged himself across the floor a few feet before coming to a rest.

"Oh my…," Ivy said. "What's happened to him?"

"Randall?" Julian was bending over Randall's prone figure.

Randall mustered the energy to lift his head, and his eyes stared around wildly. He lifted himself uneasily then slumped onto his side on the floor, half in the common room and half in the foyer. An unsteady arm lifted from his side and he pointed toward the others. His finger wobbled, then fixed squarely on Olivia. Her eyes widened, and she took one step back. Randall mouthed unintelligible words, managing only a hoarse, raspy groan. With his finger still pointing at Olivia, he heaved once more and gasped in a ragged breath, "Wa… her," before tipping over like a lead weight and crumbled prostrate on the floor. As his body settled, his other hand, clenched from the struggles, now slackened, and the remnants of a half-eaten cinnamon roll tumbled onto the carpet. He did not move again.

Four

THE DAY'S DOWNWARD trajectory steepened as I waited alone on the porch facing the roundabout. Deputy Todd Newman, the town's local authority, arrived not long after my call, and now puttered around inside, no doubt muttering to himself about all the trouble I'd caused since arriving in town less than a year ago.

I'd taken a moment to step outside and gather my thoughts. My guests, and Greta, remained inside where it was warm and dry, as the dreary weather had started up after such a promising outlook that morning. I blew out my lips, shivering slightly from the cold air, and spotted Angie, bundled up in her winter coat, rushing along the sidewalk and up to the house. Her tiny legs worked frantically, and once she made it up the steps and onto the porch, she tipped back her hood and let out a mighty sigh.

"What on earth?" she asked. "I saw Deputy Todd drive by the bakery and rushed right over."

"It's not good," I said. "One of my guests has died. This is pretty much the worst grand opening ever."

"Oh no." Angie, ever the sympathetic and comforting soul, reached up laid a hand on my shoulder, then pulled me in for a hug. She barely came up to my armpits. "I'm so sorry. I know you've worked so hard for this opening."

I wanted to cry, and Angie's sweet voice almost made it worse. "I can't seem to win here, Angie. I don't know what I'm doing wrong."

"It's not you," she said, rubbing my arm. "Accidents happen."

The squeal of tires brought our attention back to the roundabout. Harper's mail truck skidded on the wet asphalt as she pumped the brakes. Jumping out even before it came to a complete stop, the look on her face meant Harper had something to share. And it wouldn't be good. More bad news was not what I needed.

"Have you heard about Jim Thorn-in-my-side?" she asked, waving her arms wildly.

"What's wrong?" Angie asked.

Harper stomped up the stairs to the porch. "Our favorite former mayor has a new job. *County Liaison*, whatever that is. Gah, it's like he can't just let it go. He lost the election. No one likes him. Why doesn't he just leave town and spare us his presence?" Harper stopped to take a breath and noticed our forlorn faces. "Yeesh, who died?"

"Harper!" Angie admonished. "One of Poppy's guests did die."

"You're kidding me?" She looked confused, but caught on to our mood quickly when we didn't respond. When her eyes landed on Deputy Todd's truck, she must have realized we weren't kidding. "It was just a figure of speech, sorry.”

"It's all right," I said. "I'd rather talk about Jim Thornen than my dead guest, anyway."

"Where are all your guests? Have they gone home already?"

"No. They're inside with Deputy Todd where it's dry. I'm sure an ambulance will be here shortly."

"Are they going to stay?"

I sighed and leaned back against the wall. "I don't know."

"Oh, Poppy," Angie wailed. "I'll bake you a pie and that will make it all better."

"Thanks." It probably would, knowing Angie's pies, but it wouldn't take away the fact that a man died, almost literally in my arms, only moments ago. I shook my head to get the thought out of my mind. "Tell me about Jim. What's happened?"

"Ugh," Harper scoffed. "Lovie's just told me that Jim's taken a new job as a county liaison. Apparently, he'll be *liaising* with Starry Cove, knee-deep in all our business *on behalf of the county*. It's ridiculous. We didn't even receive notification."

"To be fair," Angie said, "you wouldn't have been notified—Mayor Dewey would have."

Harper sulked and waved Angie off. "Yes, but I open all his mail. He doesn't have thumbs, remember?" She wiggled her gloved hands in front of her face as if to demonstrate.

"And," Harper said, her voice straining at the mere thought, "when I dropped off mail at the hardware store, Trevor said Jim wants to join SCAT. It's unthinkable. I can't have the former mayor on the Starry Cove Action

Team—he'll ruin everything."

Angie and I shared an awkward glance before I ventured to say, "Maybe he could help."

Harper's jaw worked in silent protest as she looked from me to Angie and back.

"What she means is," Angie started, "maybe Jim can help with some menial things, so you and Dewey can get to the big stuff, like fixing the crumbling sidewalk."

"Or the overgrown bushes in the roundabout."

"Overgrown… crumbling…" Harper gaped, seemingly wounded. "I cannot believe what I am hearing."

"Forget it," I said quickly. "I'm sure Jim's just trying to be a pebble in our proverbial shoe. Let's change the topic. I spoke with Ryan today."

"Oh goodie." Angie's round face lit up, and she clapped her pudgy hands silently. "How did it go?"

"You're hot and steamy again, I hope?"

"It was never hot and steamy, trust me. I found out his son's been acting out, so he's coming to live with him here in Starry Cove. Ryan just wants some time."

"That's why he's been avoiding you?" Harper's eyes narrowed. "Pretty lame, if you ask me."

"I don't know," said Angie. "I can understand, in a way. It must be hard for him, being a widower and all. The good news is that you two are talking again."

"I guess you can call it that."

Before I could continue, the door to the house opened and Deputy Todd stepped out. The oversized sheriff's hat he wore made his lanky form seem even slighter. He tipped the rim of the hat at us and strode up, a look of utter annoyance spread across his face. "Well, well, well. Here we are again, Miss Lewis. Just when I think things are settling down in this small, sleepy town, you manage to stir up more trouble."

"She's not stirring up trouble," Angie sputtered. "Someone dying isn't trouble."

"Yeah," Harper said, sneering. "Don't blame Poppy for all the bad things that happen under your watch."

I ignored Deputy Todd's insinuation. "Do you know what happened to him?"

"Can't say for certain." He rocked back on his heels and tucked his thumbs into his belt loops. "Appears he may have choked on a cinnamon roll."

It was Angie's turn to be speechless. Her eyes grew wide, and she nearly choked on her own tongue. "My cinnamon rolls?" She looked up at me with her brown puppy dog eyes, clearly wanting me to refute what the deputy had said, but all I did was bite my lip.

"I didn't want to say anything," I said.

"He… he choked on my rolls?" she asked again, her entire body wilting in disbelief.

"Again," said Deputy Todd, "can't say for certain. We'll have to wait for the autopsy results."

Angie fidgeted with her hands. "I killed him," she whispered. "It was me. My baking actually killed a man." She turned to Harper and me frantically. "What am I going to do?"

"It's an accident, Angie, remember?" Harper turned to Deputy Todd. "It's an accident, right?"

"I'm not saying anything for certain."

My arm slid protectively around Angie as she trembled on the verge of tears. "Deputy," I said, "I told you Randall pointed right at Olivia Rivera as he came down the stairs. What about that?"

"The others mentioned that, too," he said. "It will all go into my report." My mouth opened to nudge another word in, but he held up a hand. "Now, you ladies need to clear out—not you, Miss Lewis—the ambulance is on the way. We'll know soon enough what killed Randall Portsmouth."

Five

I PREPARED TO serve up breakfast the next day to a somber crowd. No one seemed interested in small talk and, much like the previous night, most kept to themselves or whispered briefly under their breath. Not exactly the exuberant first morning meal I wanted to kick off my grand opening.

Greta hustled about, unperturbed by the recent departure of Randall's soul, preparing a concoction she referred to as "Eggs Greta," which looked suspiciously like Eggs Benedict made with French toast stacked on a waffle instead of a plain English muffin. I couldn't figure out how she whipped up masterful dishes when everything else about her remained course and unrefined. And here I was, willing and ready to learn the elegant art of cooking, but couldn't manage toast without setting off the smoke alarms and spending the rest of the day airing out the entire house.

I peered over Greta's shoulder. She stood on her little wooden stool in front of the counter, preparing the plates.

"Do you pour syrup on that, too, or just hollandaise?"

Greta smirked. "Neither."

"Neither?"

"Nope," she said, lifting her chin with pride. "I make my own holly-daisy sticky sap sauce."

"I'm scared to ask."

"Don't bother. Secret family recipe."

"You have a lot of those."

"And have I done you wrong once?"

"No," I admitted. "Everything you make has been fantastic. Although there was that one time with the brownies..."

Greta held up a free hand but continued plating. "Those were satisfied customers, I'll remind you."

I had to give her that much. It's not every day you serve the deputy sheriff's wife pot-laced brownies, but Lovie left that meeting in a rather amorous mood. And I didn't exactly hear Deputy Todd complaining, either.

"I wish my current guests were in a better mood."

"Maybe I could—"

"No," I said, cutting her off. "No more brownies."

Dejected, Greta turned back to the task at hand and grated the last dash of nutmeg over the plates. "These are ready to go," she said. "Let's go quickly before the sauce congeals."

"Congeals?"

"Quickly!"

I grabbed two plates, and we stepped into our rehearsed dance of swiveling through the kitchen door into the dining room, like two odd ballerinas, and placed my two dishes in front of Julian and Candace, who sat next to him.

"I must say," Julian said, "with everything that's happened, you don't have to go through all of this trouble for us."

"Nonsense," I replied. "You still need a good breakfast."

"My goodness, what is this?" Candace rubbed her hands together. "Looks delicious."

Yeardley leaned over to get a better look at Candace's plate. "This wasn't made by the same person who made those cinnamon rolls, was it? I don't want to keel over like Randall."

"Er, no," I said, wincing.

Candace rolled her eyes and unfurled her napkin, resting it neatly in her ample lap. "You ate one of those cinnamon rolls yesterday, remember? And you're still here."

Yeardley lowered her voice, but I could still hear her. "I could only eat one—they were bone dry. I had to swallow an entire mug of coffee with every bite."

That made me wince. I'd always known Angie's baking to be above reproach. "This is something Greta put together."

Greta beamed as she set her plates down in front of Ivy and Olivia.

Ivy stared at the eggs and put a gentle hand to her lips. "I don't know how any of you can eat at a time like this."

Olivia scoffed and snatched up her fork. "Don't be such a ninny, Ivy. You're the only one who's mourning, can't you tell?"

Ivy didn't respond, and by the time Greta and I returned with the remaining plates, the table was lively with protestations and declarations of who cared, or didn't care enough, about Randall. Greta, thankfully, put down the remaining breakfast dishes without a peep, although she still had a smug grin on her face from the previous compliment.

"God rest his soul," William said, "but I, for one, won't miss the sight of him."

"I suspect none of us will." Olivia stabbed at the eggs, letting their runny yolks ooze over the toast and waffle.

Yeardley drew back, offended. "That's a harsh thing to say. Randall wasn't the nicest person, but he's dead and we shouldn't talk ill of the dead. And don't think we didn't all see him pointing right at you. Why would he do that?"

More than a few uncomfortable pairs of eyes shifted Olivia's way, and she opened her mouth to respond, but a firm voice at the end of the table stopped her.

"That's enough." Julian sat up in his chair, exasperated. "Let's enjoy the meal our gracious hosts have provided and discuss our next steps."

"What next steps?" Ivy asked. "Surely we're leaving after this."

At this point all guests spoke at once, their voices raised up, trying to be heard over the others. Greta and I busied ourselves with the coffee and tea canisters on the buffet. I felt awkward as an audience to this conversation, but Greta hummed to herself, seemingly oblivious, until she leaned over and, between hums, whispered, "Annoying bunch, these ones."

I sighed and continued opening tea bags to fill the large brew pot.

The voices finally quieted down, and Julian continued, "We've made a promise to this town and I know we've all spent many hours delving into their past, so we'll continue with our efforts. Everett, you mentioned to me before that Randall briefed you on his research for tonight. Would you mind taking on his group of residents?"

Everett, who had mostly remained silent, dabbed the corners of his mouth with his napkin. "Of course, although, assuming I can read his handwriting, I'd like a chance to review his notes ahead of—"

A sputtering gag shocked me out of my eavesdropping. I turned from my task to see Yeardley clutching at her throat and hacking, eyes wide, face red.

Ivy stood in a rush, the dining chair clattering to the floor behind her. "Not her, too!"

The others reacted in a less dramatic fashion. Some held their breath and Julian even gasped. Everyone was still on edge from the previous day, it seemed.

"Relax," Candace said, slapping Yeardley firmly on the back. "She's taken a bite down the wrong pipe."

A thwack boomed as Candace took another swing. Color returned to Yeardley's face after the wallop brought up whatever had blocked her windpipe, and the table settled down with shared looks of embarrassment at their reactions.

"She's all right," Candace said, rubbing Yeardley's back where she'd hit the hardest. "Just needs a minute."

Yeardley smiled weakly and took a drink of water. "I'm sorry, everyone. I thought I was a goner there for a second."

"That's all right," Julian said. "Everett, would you continue?"

Everett's eyes were still on Yeardley. No doubt worried she'd have another fit, but he soon picked up where he had left off. "I'll do my best, but I cannot guarantee I'll be able to share the levels of detail Randall would have."

"That's understandable," Julian said. "I'm sure everyone will appreciate whatever you can provide. His notes are with me—they boxed them up when…" Julian's voice trailed off, leaving the rest unsaid.

Everett seemed not to notice or care. "I'd also like a chance to review the church's records while we're here."

"Me too," said William. "In fact, I'd hoped for a presentation there tomorrow, if the pastor will agree."

"I'm sure he will," I said without thinking. I'd forgotten my task at the buffet and only now realized I had been listening to their conversation fully and without any attempt to conceal it. Their heads all swiveled my way.

"That's what I want to hear," William said, smiling through his scraggly beard.

"Excellent," Everett said, "then there are the town's own records. I suspect those would be kept by the mayor."

Candace almost spit out her orange juice. "You might be out of luck," she said with a chuckle. "Haven't you heard? The town's mayor is a cat."

"A cat?" Ivy repeated, but no one paid her any mind.

Everett's lip twitched in irritation. "No matter. Someone's bound to know where they're kept. And perhaps," his eyes flicked my direction, "there are some records in this old house?"

"I have a library." My hand drifted in the direction of the door off the foyer. "You're welcome to it any time.

I'd love to know if you find anything of interest."

Greta grunted in protest. As she saw it, the library was hers, and any intrusion without her permission was an affront.

"And if anyone else is looking for something interesting today, my friend's bakery is having a little celebration."

"Cinnamon rolls?" Yeardley asked, but Candace placed a hand on her arm to shush her.

"Er, yes," I said, stumbling over the words. "But it's an award-winning bakery. In fact, we're celebrating a magazine article about it that comes out today."

"That sounds lovely, dear." Candace smiled sweetly and patted Yeardley on the arm. "We'll try to pop over at some point."

No one else offered to come by. My shoulders sagged as I scanned the group, worried for Angie. If word got around—and word would definitely get around—her bakery's reputation could be in trouble.

Breaking the awkward silence, Olivia said, "If we're staying after all, then we should talk more details about tonight's presentation."

"Ah, yes," Julian said. "Poppy, I hate to ask at your own table, but would you and your assistant excuse us?" He tapped the side of his nose and smiled. "Confidential discussion."

"Of course," I said, grabbing the ripped and discarded tea bags and a soiled towel off the buffet. "Greta?" I motioned for her to follow me out.

"Everything was an absolute delight," Candace gushed as we disappeared into the kitchen, leaving the guests to their private conversation.

"What a nightmare," I said to Greta after the swivel door came to a stop behind us. "Angie's bakery is doomed if anyone suspects her food is killing people."

"I thought the old man, you know…" Greta grabbed at her throat and stuck her tongue out. "Choked."

"It won't matter. If he'd slipped on her cinnamon roll and fell to his death instead, she'd still be considered suspect. This town is like that."

"Well," Greta said, shrugging and turning away, "if there's nothing else, I'm going to hunker down in the library."

"Just a minute."

Greta stopped mid-step and turned back toward me. "Have you found anything yet? Anything at all?"

"That depends on your definition of 'anything.'"

I took a deep breath and caught myself gnashing my teeth. "Anything that would be helpful in deciphering the map we found scrawled on the frame of one of the antique—and valuable—Victorian chairs that I now have stashed in my private room because you ripped open the upholstery."

"Ah," Greta muttered, avoiding my eyes while she smoothed the wrinkles in her drab gray dress. "In that case, no. It doesn't match anything so far."

I expected this answer, which is why I used it to lead into my next point. "In that case, I think it's time we branch out."

"Branch out?"

"That's right." I tried to sound casual, flitting over to the window above the sink and pretended to rearrange my collection of ceramic birds perched on the sill. "Branch out to other sources."

When I turned back, Greta had worked her mouth into a crooked frown.

"I got you something," I said.

She waited a moment in silence and then asked in a whisper, "What's your definition of 'something'?"

"A library card." I pulled a plastic card from my back pocket and held it out to her.

She didn't take it. "I already have a library."

"This is to the *real* library. The big one in Vista."

"But Arthur's books are more important. They're his life's work. His personal collection. They've got to hold the answers."

"Apparently not," I said. "You've scoured that entire collection by now and, by your own admission, you've found nothing."

"I may have misinterpreted—"

"Nothing," I repeated, still holding out the card.

Greta wilted.

"And there's another thing."

Greta wilted further, if that was possible.

"An incentive."

Her ears perked up, and she raised a graying eyebrow.

This was the kicker. I knew she wouldn't be able to resist. "If you promise to be very careful, I will let you take the scooter to the library in Vista."

Greta snatched the card from my hands before I could blink and squirreled it away in the folds of her dress. "I promise."

A satisfied grin spread across my face. "You will take the Coastal Road only—no highway for that little scooter."

Greta nodded.

"You will not speed and you will wear a helmet at all times."

Greta nodded again and hopped from foot to foot. "Yes, yes. I promise. When can I go?"

"I'm stopping by Angie's bakery before you go anywhere. Why don't you gather and wash any dishes upstairs and clean up after breakfast? I'll be back soon to help turn down the rooms."

"How long will you be gone?" Her voice bubbled with urgency.

"Don't worry, I'll be back before the library even opens. Right now, I have a feeling Angie needs my support."

***

I found Angie pacing inside the bakery. Her apron was a crumpled mess, wrinkled and filthy from being wrung by the nervous hands of a baker. The place was empty, even though the bakery opened promptly at six o'clock each morning. I'd expected more people, especially since Angie's article released today. A stack of fresh copies of *Bake Shop Bliss* sat on the counter, untouched. The baked goods display case burst with tender laminated croissants and buttery scones, but you'd have heard a cricket chirp in all the silence. Her face had lit up as the door chime announced my arrival, but once she saw it was me, it fell again.

"It's awful," she said, "just awful. No one has come by and it's nearly nine already."

"I'm sure everyone's just getting a late start. They'll come by."

Angie let her head fall back and released a heaving sigh. Chubby hands picked up her apron and gave it another tight wring. It twisted into a knot, like a security blanket into which she could channel all her fears.

"Let me see the magazine." I tried to add a little cheer to my voice, a little pep to get her excited about the article.

She trudged back behind the counter and I met her there, reaching for the top copy and pulled it off the stack. I let out a delighted squeak. "I didn't know you'd be on the cover." I held the magazine up in front of me with an enormous grin on my face, as if she hadn't seen the cover yet. A glossy rounded face with rosy cherub cheeks and warm, vibrant eyes smiled out at unseen readers. "Pies the Limit," I said, reading aloud the article title emblazoned next to her lovable visage. "It's so cute."

"That just makes it worse."

I gave her my best smile and said, "Buck up, Angie. This could be the greatest moment of your career."

Angie frowned and looked toward the window at the gloomy morning outside. A few pans clattered in the kitchen, but otherwise there was no burble of excitement or chattering of celebrating patrons. Her eyes, welling with tears, met mine and I winced.

"It's the cinnamon rolls," she said after a moment. "No one wants to eat here because of that cinnamon roll debacle with your guests." She covered her face with her hands.

"How could anyone know about that? It's such a minor detail."

"Minor detail?" She repeated through tears. "Don't you remember who suggested it? Deputy Todd. Deputy

Todd Newman, married to Lovie Newman, town chatterbox and celebrated gossip. I'd be surprised if the whole county doesn't suspect my cinnamon rolls by now."

"It wasn't your cinnamon rolls."

"How do you know?" Deep creases of worry marred her face. "What if it was, Poppy? What if Roy comes home to find out that I'm in prison? A felon. Wasting away in the big house for the rest of my life. Instead of making banana bread, I'll be making license plates."

"That won't happen."

She spread her stubby arms wide. "Look around. No one is here for a reason. A few months ago, people couldn't stop talking about my pies and the upcoming article. Now? My bakery is a ghost town." She dabbed at her tears with the corner of her apron. "A wasteland of butter and flour."

"It's the lady of the hour," Harper announced with a boom in her voice as she strode into the bakery. "The queen of the moment. The pride of the…" Harper's voice died down when she spotted our faces. "What? Did someone else die?"

"Just my livelihood," Angie said sourly. "And my reputation."

"Angie thinks no one is here because of what happened with my guest and her cinnamon rolls."

"What? That's crazy. He was some old guy, right? He was probably ready to kick the bucket, anyway." Harper helped herself to coffee and plopped down at the only table. "No one could possibly think your cinnamon rolls killed anybody."

At that moment, the bakery door chimed again. Our heads swiveled to see who had arrived, then Angie let out a strangled gurgle. Veronica Valentine's instantly recognizable harsh blonde bob and scrawny frame filled the doorway. The *Vista View* newspaper reporter honed in on Angie's plump figure behind the counter and her eyes narrowed behind red-rimmed glasses. A sly grin spread across her face. "Angie Owens," she said, whipping out a recorder from a hidden pocket in her jacket. "Just who I came to see."

Harper popped out of her chair, and we both quickly maneuvered ourselves between Veronica and our friend. Angie whimpered softly behind us.

"What do you want?" Harper demanded.

"Me?" Veronica responded in a honeyed voice. "I'm here to interview Mrs. Owens. I understand she has a magazine releasing today. Perhaps I was mistaken."

She turned to leave, but Angie's voice squeaked out, "You're… you're here about the magazine?"

Veronica's grin spread further across her face, the sharp lines deepening. "Of course," she said, using her arms to clear a path through me and Harper. "Why else would I be here? Hmm?"

I shared a wary look with Harper, but the glimmer of hope in Angie's voice held me back from throwing Veronica out of the bakery and onto her backside. Few positive news stories flowed from Veronica Valentine's pen, and fewer still failed to include at least a snippet of scandalous intrigue, true or not.

"My, my, this must be it here." Veronica clawed at the stack of *Bake Shop Bliss* with her red-lacquered nails. "So charming. Now," she said, holding up the recorder to capture her words, "tell my readers what it's like to be a famous baker. Is it all cakes and pies, or do things sometimes get… sticky?"

"Oh," Angie tittered, "I'm not famous. It's just an article about my pies. I won the—"

"Yes, your pies. But that isn't all you're known for, now is it?"

"Well, the pies won me the—"

"You prepare a variety of other confections, don't you, Mrs. Owens?" Veronica's voice was sugar. "You have a *specialty*, isn't that so?"

Angie's voice wavered. "A specialty?"

"That's right. I heard that not only are you a famous pie artist, but you're also well known for your *cinnamon rolls*."

Horror overtook Angie's features. Like a trapped rabbit, I could almost see her heart rate rise as she searched for an escape.

"That's enough," Harper said, grabbing at Veronica's arms, but the reporter slipped out of her grasp.

"Are you concerned the magazine will retract their story?"

"Retract their story?" Angie repeated as if she didn't understand the words.

I reached for Veronica's recorder, but she ducked and crawled over a chair at the table before dragging it between us to cut me off.

"Now that your cinnamon rolls have been implicated in the death of Randall Portsmouth."

"You crispy-haired crone," Harper spat. "Angie's got nothing to hide."

"My readership has the right to know."

"Know what?" I asked. "That an old man died? So what?"

"That's pretty flippant for you, Poppy Lewis, considering it was your house, once again, playing host to a mysterious death. I don't suppose you'd like to say anything on the record."

I scoffed. "There's nothing mysterious about it."

"I hear differently—and from reliable sources, at that."

"Who?" Harper boomed. "Lovie Newman?"

Veronica snapped her mouth shut, effectively confirming the accusation.

"Lovie Newman is about as reliable as your journalistic integrity." Harper crossed her arms defiantly. "I would hate for a strongly worded letter to make its way from the desk of the Mayor of Starry Cove to the Editor of the *Vista View* accusing one of its *junior* reporters of harassment."

"Ha!" Veronica cackled. "I'd like to see that. A letter from a cat. We'd likely publish it on the front page."

Harper growled and lunged for Veronica, but I held out a firm arm to stop her. "I think that's enough." I turned back to Veronica. "If you aren't here to cover the magazine article, then you aren't welcome."

"Fine." Veronica's voice was back to honey as she clicked the recorder back on. "Local girl strikes gold baking pies." She glanced at Angie, then whispered, "And taking lives."

"Why you—" Harper sprang at the reporter, and the skinny woman dashed for the door. But as she reached for the handle, a woman with gray-blonde curls pushed it open.

"What on earth is going on here?" Lovie stopped in mid-stride and peered around at the commotion. Angie sobbed behind the counter. Harper seethed against a chair like a wild animal. Strands of bleached-blonde hair stuck out sideways from Veronica's head. The only sound in the room was the echo of the fading door chime.

"Nothing," I said. "Good morning."

Lovie sniffed, but allowed the door to close behind her. "I thought I'd stop by—"

"For the magazine release?" I heard the desperation in my voice.

"No," Lovie said, avoiding Angie's gaze. "I thought you'd all like to hear the news."

Veronica stepped closer and thrust the recorder into Lovie's face. "What news?"

"Well," Lovie said, speaking into the recorder, "apparently the Treasures of the Coast gift shop has a new owner." She waited with a knowing smile for our reactions.

"Who the heck would want to buy that ratty old place?"

"And what are they planning to do with it?" I asked. "It's full of junk." The sprawling shop on the Coastal Road just outside of town had remained empty since its previous owner met with a rather untimely demise. I couldn't imagine anyone would want to take it over.

"They bought it part and parcel, or so Beatrice's nephew's next-door neighbor at the county offices says."

"So, you know this fifth-hand?" Harper crossed her arms and leveled a look of satisfaction directly at Veronica.

"No," Lovie said matter-of-factly. "I know this fourth-hand. *You* know this fifth-hand." She waved Harper off and continued. "Anyway, all I know is a name:

Charlie something-or-other."

"And will Charlie something-or-other be at the town meeting tonight? The mayor might want to make an announcement."

Lovie bristled at Harper's attitude. "I just told you that was all I knew. If you want to find out more, you should go out to the shop yourself and find out."

"Maybe I'll just do that."

"Good," Lovie said with a nod, "and when you get back be sure to come by the diner and tell me everything because I've got to run. Lots to do." She began for the door. "Toodles." And with a wiggle of her fingers and a ring of the door chime, Lovie was gone.

"I've got to run, too," said Veronica. She stuffed the recorder back into the pocket of her jacket, but as she opened the bakery door, she stopped and turned back to us. With a fiery twinkle in her eye, she said, "Thanks for the exclusive, ladies. See you tonight."

"Ugh," said Harper after the door closed behind Veronica. "I could strangle that woman, but she'd just slither out of my hands again."

"What do you think she'll write about my bakery?"

"She can't print lies, Angie."

"But she can speculate. That's all people need."

Tears welled in Angie's weary eyes and my jaw tightened. This cinnamon roll debacle could sully her reputation, threaten her livelihood, and unfairly punish the kindest woman I knew. I couldn't just sit and watch it play out.

"I need to go," I said. "I need to get back and help Greta." I gave Angie a tight squeeze. "We'll sort it out, Angie. I promise."

Six

JULIAN WAS BUNDLED up tight against the cold, which is probably why we crashed into one another on the side-walk outside the bakery. With his wool scarf blowing into his face, I don't think he saw me, and with my mind elsewhere, I didn't see him either.

"I'm so sorry," I said, hoisting the elderly man up off the pavement. "I wasn't looking."

"Neither was I," he said, yanking the scarf out of his face and brushing off his pants. "My apologies."

"Are you all right?"

"Yes, I'm fine. Don't worry about me. I was trying to find the bakery you mentioned this morning."

I let excitement overtake me. "For the magazine re-lease? It's right here." I pointed to the door nearby. "An-gie—that's my friend—will be so happy if you stop by. It's been pretty slow this morning and you'll definitely lift her spirits."

"Gladly. And then I need to find someone who can discuss preparation for tonight's event. I don't suppose your mayor would be much help."

"You'll want to talk to Harper Tillman. She's sort of like Mayor Dewey's handler. And you're in luck—she's at the bakery right now. Tall, thin Black woman. She's wearing a Postal Service uniform. And she's also the only other person in the bakery right now."

Julian thought for a moment, then asked, "Did she take part in the genealogy event? I don't remember any-one with that description."

I responded with a drawn out, "No," before adding, "Not her thing, apparently."

"That's too bad. I wish more people with our heritage would delve into their family histories. There is still a lot to be learned, despite the difficulties."

"You're welcome to ask her. I'm sure you have a gentle way with people. At least, the group seem to re-spect you a lot." I peered at the purple mansion looming behind him in the distance. "How are they holding up?"

"About as well as can be expected. Randall wasn't, ah, the most popular member of our little society. Rubbed people the wrong way more often than not. To be quite frank, most of us tolerated him at best."

"Yeah, I caught on to that."

Julian made an apologetic face. "I'm terribly sorry this happened. I know the whole thing is an inconven-ience."

"Inconvenience?" I nearly tripped over the word, astonished that he worried about me at a time like this. "You lost a member of your club."

"It is very sad," he said and dug his hands into the woolen pockets of his jacket. "Randall was a genius, in his own way."

"Did anyone dislike him enough to, you know, do something terrible?"

Julian's eyes widened for just a moment. "I'm not sure what happened to Randall, and I was probably the only one who could stand him, even a little—that's why I asked you to pair us as roommates. But, no." He shook his head, "No, I can't imagine anyone would do anything to harm him."

"Has anyone been acting strange at all?" My eyes pleaded. "My friend's under suspicion. Her bakery. The cinnamon rolls…"

"Well, it couldn't have been anything to do with the cinnamon rolls. Yeardley herself ate at least one." He stopped in thought. "Actually, now that you mention it, Yeardley has been very secretive lately. I think she may be working on a manuscript. I've seen her scribbling here and there, but she won't show it to anyone."

"What kind of manuscript?" I asked.

He blew out a sigh and a puff of warm breath floated away. "Like I said, she won't show it to anyone. I suspect she worried Randall would steal her research."

"Why would he do that?"

"Because he's Randall."

"And what does—"

"Good morning, Miss Lewis." Deputy Todd's voice twanged from behind me and my face drooped.

"I'll leave you to it," Julian said with a grin. He tucked his scarf into the collar of his jacket and left toward the bakery as I turned to face Deputy Todd. Usually, I'd cringe, but I had a few words to share with the deputy this morning.

"Good morning to you, too," I said. "I hope you've

come by to share good news."

He hooked his thumbs into his belt loops and rocked back on his heels. His large nose twitched like a rabbit, and his bushy mustache twitched along with it. No forthright response meant there was no good news to be had.

"I don't share details with civilians, Miss Lewis."

"That's ridiculous," I said flatly. "You share details all the time."

Deputy Todd grumbled and stopped rocking. "I don't have any news, if that's what you're after."

I scowled and pursed my lips. "You know Angie's not a part of this. She wouldn't hurt a fly and her cinnamon rolls are the best in the county."

"Now I'm not saying she's a murderess, Miss Lewis. All I'm saying is that Randall Portsmouth had a half-eaten cinnamon roll in his hand when he died."

I stepped closer to the deputy. "Maybe he just choked. And Yeardley ate them, too. She didn't have any adverse effects. Have you talked to her? What about underlying health conditions? We know nothing about Randall's habits or medical issues or if he was just one tedious eye roll away from a stroke."

Deputy Todd held up his hands. "Enough, Miss Lewis."

Deep breath. I let the cold air fill my lungs. It couldn't be Angie, it just couldn't. My shoulders sagged. "You can't do this to her."

"I can't rule out the chance that Randall died because of her cinnamon roll. Accidental or not."

"But she may not have even made them!" I clapped my hands over my mouth. Stupid, stupid, stupid.

Deputy Todd's eyebrows shot up. "What are you

saying Miss Lewis?"

I shook my head vigorously. Ugh! Why did I open my big mouth? "Nothing. I just meant that… What I mean is…"

"Out with it."

"No, no, it's nothing. Please forget I said anything. I'm sure Randall just choked, right?"

Deputy Todd grunted. "We'll see about that," he said, tipping his wide sheriff's hat. "See you tonight, Miss Lewis."

***

I found Greta in one of the upstairs rooms. She'd already stripped away the bed linen and tossed them into the hamper when I joined her, picking up the corner of the sheet and helping her finish tucking in the corners.

"You're late," she said. "I didn't realize you meant I could take the scooter out next year."

"I'm not late. I told you I'd be back after I stopped to see Angie."

"Suit yourself. I thought you wanted me to do more research, but if you want to lollygag at the bakery, by all means."

Greta continued to straighten up the room, avoiding eye contact and occasionally huffing to ensure I noticed her displeasure.

"You mentioned that the map we found on the chair doesn't match any known location."

A grunt was the only response. I took it as an affirmative reply.

"What if it isn't a location, though?"

Greta's head popped from behind a folding screen, a

few strands of her gray hair hung loose and wild, while the rest was tucked back into a messy bun. "What do you mean?"

I shook my head, tired and dismissive of my own thoughts. "I don't know. I'm just thinking. Trying to riddle it out."

"It looked like a map."

I agreed. The scrawl we found underneath the upholstery looked every bit a map, but to what, we didn't know. It wasn't like there was a pointer saying "You are here" with a clearly delineated path to buried treasure. It was just a bunch of lines and dots. And what about those cryptic words Harper and I had discovered in an underground tomb? *Only those born of golden blood may possess the riches borne from blood.*

"Whatever it means," I said, "at least the Gold Hand don't have it."

Greta's face crinkled at the name. The Gold Hand, a shadowy group we knew little about, had been hot on our heels searching the same vague promise of treasure. I'd avoid another run in with them at all cost.

"They'll know that the treasure isn't in that dilapidated and deserted forest town. And," Greta continued with a self-satisfied smile, "they don't have your secret weapon."

I scoffed. "What secret weapon?"

"Me," she said, grinning like a cat who'd caught a mouse.

I opened my mouth to reply, but her eyes shifted to behind me toward the door. I turned my head to find Everett leaning against the door jamb, leg crossed casually over the other, watching me and Greta. "Hello," he said once we'd noticed him. "I'm just waiting for the room to be ready."

"Of course," I said, grabbing at a towel laid across the back of a chair. "We're all done here. Greta, grab the hamper."

She took hold of the rolling hamper and spun in out of the door past Everett, who made way for us to pass. He thanked me as I stepped through the door and closed it behind us. I let out a heaving sigh.

"We've got to be more careful. I have to remember random people walk around my house now."

"He didn't hear anything."

"How do you know?" I asked.

"I don't, but if I heard what we were talking about, I'd be asking some questions."

"That's because you're nosy."

Greta scowled and pushed the hamper toward the next room. But when I opened the door, Yeardley stood up quickly from her spot on the bed. A notebook was clutched in one hand, loose pages jutted out from all angles, pages which must have been pieced together or added later.

"Sorry," I said, still surprised to find her there. "I thought everyone was out and about in town already."

Yeardley snapped the notebook shut and pawed at a bag laying on the bed before shoving the notebook inside. "I just need to…" She peered around, first at the bed, then at the side table before spotting what she was looking for. She snatched a small medicine bottle off the table and shoved it into the bag as well.

Greta and I waited as she fumbled.

"My blood pressure medicine," was all she said,

turning sideways to pass us as she left the room. Her footsteps faded down the staircase and Greta and I exchanged a look of curiosity.

"Julian mentioned that Yeardley's been secretive about a manuscript she's been working on. I bet that was it."

Greta exhaled with a whoosh and cackled. "I thought she was gonna pee herself when we came in. Hoo-ey! I've been there before, let me tell you."

"Please don't," I grumbled.

"And it ain't pretty."

Seven

I STEPPED OVER several residents and only squashed one set of toes getting to my seat next to Angie at the town meeting.

"Wow," I said, plopping into the chair. "I can't remember the last time the community center was this full."

"Ginger Dobrowski's wedding reception," Angie replied, tugging on her jacket stuck between the stackable chairs.

"Ah, yes," I said, remembering. "Open bar."

"I had to drag Roy home while he sang love ballads from the Eighties at the top of his lungs."

"Sounds romantic."

Angie grunted. "At least the cake was beautiful."

"Of course it was," I said. "You made it."

"And everyone ate it." Angie glanced around the room. "Look at them now. They won't touch my baking. And you know what?"

"What?"

"Deputy Todd had the nerve to come into the bakery

today and ask about Cesar making cinnamon rolls. Cesar, of all people, can you believe that?"

I hid my shameful grimace from Angie and hoped Deputy Todd's line of inquiry went nowhere.

"Well," Angie said with a huff, "I put a stop to that lickety-split. Wanted to know what goes into the rolls, that type of thing, as if I'm going to share my recipe with just anyone. Oh look, there's Shelby." Angie waved her hand to catch Shelby's attention. I spied the beehive wobbling through the crowd, but she didn't come our way. "She's ignoring me, too," Angie said, sighing. "We're doing a test run for the catering business. She's prepared her savory bites tonight and she won't even look at me."

"I'm sure she's just busy."

"She doesn't want to associate with my tainted buns." Angie crossed her arms and huddled deeper into her chair. She swung her dangling feet back and forth and seemed to stew on the inside.

Hoping to set a more cheerful course of conversation, I asked, "I saw one of my guests headed to the bakery this morning. Did he stop in?"

Angie's pout transitioned into a smile. It wasn't in her nature to be sad. "Yes, he did. He even bought something. And I showed him the article, too. He seemed like a nice fellow."

"That was Julian. He's the leader of the society."

"I wonder what they're going to share tonight?"

"No idea," I said. "I hope there's nothing embarrassing in my family history."

"Is Greta coming?"

"Are you kidding? She'd rather poke her eye out with a blunt twig. Besides, once she got back from the library she zonked out. Probably still asleep. All the guests are here tonight, so I didn't have any reason to wake her."

Angie lowered her voice, although the milling crowd paid us no attention. "Did she find anything useful?"

"I doubt it, otherwise she'd have said something. I suspect she mostly zipped around on the Vespa instead."

"Are you sure that was a good idea? Giving Greta access to a motorized vehicle sounds like a liability."

"Giving Greta access to anything is a liability, but it's the only way to get her out of the house and she's a lot better at research than the rest of us."

Angie had to admit that much. "That's true. I get too distracted and Harper would probably fall asleep rummaging through old books for too long."

"It's not books I'm concerned about, it's the electronic databases that I want her to search."

Angie snorted. "Good luck with that. Even if she goes to the library, she's going to set up camp surrounded by books. She won't touch a computer."

"Baby steps. The first step was getting her there."

"Getting who where?" Harper appeared in the aisle next to Angie. Mayor Dewey, eyes half-lidded, purred in her arms and his ginger tail curled against her body.

"Greta to the library," I said.

Harper snorted.

Angie swiveled her eyes back on me. "That's what I said."

"We're starting soon." Harper hoisted and adjusted Dewey to a more comfortable position. "Are all your guests here, Poppy?"

I scanned the group mingling in the front of the community center's large room. Everyone was there except

Randall. A pang hit me. For a moment I'd been able to forget his recent passing. "All here," I replied.

"Greta's missing out, if you ask me," said Angie. "I think tonight will be a lot of fun. It can only make our little town more interesting."

"Not too interesting, I hope." My eyes wandered to where Veronica Valentine sat prominently in the front row, erect in her chair. Fierce blonde bobbed hair gave her away from a mile. She was speaking quickly into her hand-held recording device as she scanned the room. From my spot, I could not hear what she was saying, but it couldn't be good. Her eyes met mine, and they narrowed as she spread her blood-red lips into a devilish grin. Her muttering increased.

I groaned and turned my attention to the genealogists chattering quietly from across the room, I spied Ryan making his way down the aisle toward the front. Dark green sweater today. He was handsome in a nerdy way, like how he let his glasses slide down his nose before propping them back up with a quick flick of his forefinger. Or how he walked, lithely, but without pretension. And the imperceptible squeak of his shoes with every step, step, step. Or how he slid effortlessly into his chair and struck up a conversation with the stunning woman sitting next to him.

"Wha…" I said, shaking out of my daydream. "Who is that?" I pointed toward the woman next to Ryan. Her dark shoulder-length chestnut hair fell around her smooth, flawless face, and it waved like a shampoo commercial with every chuckle as she and Ryan chatted. They talked and smiled, and chuckled more. I never knew chuckles could be so revolting.

"Oh, her," Angie whispered. "I was going to tell you. That's Charlie Barba, the new owner of Treasures of the Coast."

"*That* is Charlie?"

Harper let out a low whistle. "She's a looker."

"I was expecting something different."

"Like what?" Angie asked.

"I don't know," I said. "Maybe a Y chromosome, I guess."

"She came into the bakery earlier today. She's very nice, even congratulated me on the magazine feature."

My eyes hadn't left the sight of Charlie and Ryan talking, and Angie must have noticed. "I'm sure he's just being friendly," she said. "He was one of the first to greet you when you moved here, remember?"

"Yeah," I said, "right before he asked me out on a date."

"Don't worry about it," said Harper. "Ryan's not that kind of guy."

Angie nodded emphatically. "That's right."

"And, if he turns out to be," Harper continued, eyes narrowing, "it's Team Poppy, all the way."

"Team Poppy," Angie agreed, continuing to nod.

Teams. I was never any good at competition. Like that time I kicked the ball into my own goal in the Sweet Petunias soccer league when I was five. And I was always picked last at recess. Always.

My pocket vibrated as Harper and Mayor Dewey stepped up to the dais. I pulled my phone out and read the screen. Lily. I'd forgotten to call her back. Craning my neck, I searched for a viable exit, but people had taken their seats and we were locked in like sardines—there was no escape. I sent the call to voicemail just as Harper spoke.

"Welcome everyone. We've got a lot going on tonight, so settle in. First off, Mayor Dewey would like everyone to know that your concerns about the pothole in front of the hardware store are noted and will be communicated to the transportation authorities. Don't hold your breath, though, because we know how long it took them to fix the misspelled STOP painted on the road out of town.

"Second, I want to congratulate our very own Angie Owens. If you don't know—and I'm not sure what rock you've been living under—Angie's been featured in this month's *Bake Shop Bliss* magazine. Pick up a copy today and support your local baker. Yay Angie!" Harper maneuvered her hands to clap, but only jostled Dewey and slap a few lanky fingers together. The rest of the room managed a lukewarm applause, except for my own clapping echoing off the walls.

Angie's cheeks reddened, and she sank into her chair. Embarrassed by the attention or from the lack of support, I wasn't sure, but I wrapped an arm around her and gave her a squeeze. She smiled up at me with a look of pained thanks, and I knew it was the latter that had affected her so.

Harper quickly moved on to the next topic. "Deputy Todd has asked to say a few words, so… deputy?" Harper peered into the audience, but a guttural "ahem" came from the sidelines and she sidestepped away from the podium to allow Deputy Todd to saunter into the spotlight.

"Thank you, uh…" He glanced at Harper and Dewey before adding, "Mayor." Clearing his throat once more, the deputy began, "As you all may know, an emergency was called in at the Lewis residence yesterday. An adult male, Randall Portsmouth, approximately sixty years old was found unresponsive and died at the scene."

Veronica whispered into her recorder, but her emphatic gesticulations meant she was already spinning her tale for tomorrow's news article.

"We are currently awaiting autopsy results." Here he paused and glanced at the genealogists waiting somberly in the shadows. "Shouldn't take too much longer."

A tuttering from Veronica broke the silence that followed. Deputy Todd's eyes narrowed and his shoulders sagged. "A quick question," she said, "if I may, deputy."

"You may not, Miss Valentine. This isn't a press conference or a cross examination open to questioning."

She continued as if she didn't hear what he'd just said. "Are there any suspects? Anyone…"

If I hadn't been watching her directly, I might not have noticed the exaggerated dip of her head in our direction. A faint gurgle escaped next to me. Angie must have been watching as well.

"I said no questions," Deputy Todd repeated, this time more forcefully. "And who says there's something to suspect, anyway? There's nothing to report. Go about your business, all of you." He nodded once, the quick jab of his chin noting the finality of it.

"If I could ask one more—"

"No!" Deputy Todd stomped from the podium and took his seat next to Lovie where he fumed under his wide-brimmed hat.

Harper scurried to the microphone, still supporting Dewey in her arms. "Thank you, uh, Deputy Todd," she said. "The next item on the agenda before we move on to the presentation is the monthly SCAT meeting, which will be held here at the community center in three days. We'll be discussing the project goals for next quarter. Anyone is welcome. I hope to see you all there."

Jim Thornen straightened up in the front row, and Harper's face turned into a scowl. "Most of you, that is." She turned to face the group of genealogists, who stood ready to take the podium. "Now I'd like to welcome the Vista County Genealogical and Historical Society up to the front. For those of you who may not know, the Society selects a town every year and presents their ancestry research as a public service. This year, our own Starry Cove was selected. Let's give them a round of applause." As the audience clapped, Harper and Mayor Dewey receded into the shadows.

Julian pulled a pair of reading glasses from his top pocket, then rustled with a few papers on the podium and adjusted the microphone. "Good evening, Starry Cove. The Vista County Genealogical and Historical Society is pleased to be here to share our research with you. We hope you will take from this a new understanding of your heritage and the depth of your town's historical significance. We've found in our past ventures that these presentations foster a sense of community and bring people together in new and exciting ways. We hope you'll have a similar experience."

I felt like I was hearing an old story being told by my grandfather, whom I barely remembered. Julian's voice soothed me with its soft baritone and gentle cadence.

Julian continued, "We'd also like to thank Pastor Basil Meyers, who has graciously allowed us to tour and present on Starry Cove's historical church."

Someone in the audience shouted, "It ain't old!" I thought it sounded like Trevor French, the owner of the hardware store. I shared his surprise. Although it looked like an old stone church, I'd always been told the Fellowship of the Faith building was simply constructed to look old.

"Ah," Julian said and tapped the side of his nose with a knowing smile. "We invite you to join us there tomorrow night to find out the truth."

This garnered more than a few curious mumbles and shared whispers throughout the room. Even Angie and I exchanged wondering glances and Veronica murmured a few words into her recorder.

"Now, while not the oldest town in the county, Starry Cove adds to the rich history of this wild western landscape. Situated on the coast, you may not be surprised to hear that it thrived as a fishing village, or that the far-reaching forests provided the bounty of lumber that built the earliest towns of Vista County, just like your own Starry Cove. And while many of these towns faded into the history books, the people remained, building lives and families that remain here today.

"We'd like to present our most intriguing findings in two stages. First, we will speak on those families who have remained in Starry Cove throughout the generations. Then, we'll explore the special histories of new blood—those families who sought out Starry Cove and made it their new home. After that, we welcome you to meet with your assigned genealogist to delve further into your own family history."

The crowd, like me, followed Julian's every word.

He introduced the Society members one by one—each with an accompanying applause—then allowed Candace to take the podium.

"I'm so thrilled to be here," she began. "It's such an honor to present to you, so I'll dive right in to our town founders. Is there a Trevor French here tonight?"

Trevor, tall and still wearing his dusty overalls, stood up from his spot in the crowd. "I'm here," he said, waving. "Over here."

Candace spotted him quickly and gave him a satisfied smile and a nod before focusing back on her notes. "Mr. Trevor French, I am happy to say, is the descendant of one Theophilus French along his father's line, who, in the earliest records of Starry Cove, was proprietor of the local tonsorial parlor."

Trevor stared at her with a look of confusion. "The tonsil what?"

"Tonsorial parlor, Mr. French. Often referred to as a barbershop today, although Theophilus was much more than a barber. He would have been a highly respected member of society, since the tonsorial art required years and years of training."

"Gosh," Trevor said, "how about that?"

"Yes, indeed," Candace replied. "If you would like to learn more, please find me after the presentation. Next up is Ms. Georgia Landry."

Georgia, who sat in her usual chair next to Beatrice Trotter, smoothed her skirt as she stood up. "Hello," she said in a meek voice. Although she played in the bell choir at church every Sunday in front of the entire congregation, Georgia was a woman of few words, and often left conversation up to Beatrice, whom I'd rarely seen her without.

"Ah, yes, Ms. Landry." Candace nodded approvingly at Georgia before grasping a presentation remote that lay on the podium. With an exuberant click of a lacquered finger, the slideshow began. A foxed black-and-white photograph shone on the screen before the audience. A man and a woman, grizzled and hard-worn and wearing clothes that wouldn't have been out-of-place in an old western, stood together on a raised wooden walkway. Their mouths were hard lines—no cheerful smiles here—as they stared out from the picture. A simple and roughly painted sign hung from the slatted wall behind them: Provisions. "What newly established town on the frontier can do without its very own general store?"

At this, Ursula sat up straighter in her chair and stared at Georgia from across the room.

Candace continued, "None, I tell you. That's why Millicent and Ebenezer Tillingsworth, your great- great- great- grandparents opened the very first general store in Starry Cove in 1876."

Georgia perked up at this information, clearly pleased with the fortitude and gumption of her ancestors. Candace clicked to the next slide. This one, smudged along the sides, presented a very different scene. The charred remains of the same building, the sign now fallen and half-destroyed, lay in a smoldering pile of timbers on the muddy ground. The whispers that had bubbled through the crowd suddenly deflated. "Unfortunately," Candace continued, "both perished in a fiery blaze that destroyed the store and killed all but one of their children asleep in the lodgings upstairs."

Georgia lowered herself into her chair with unsteady

hands, and Beatrice laid a hand on her shoulder and whispered something into her ear. You could hear a pin drop.

Candace leaned into the microphone with a twinkle in her eye. "These old accounts are just so exciting," she said with a buzz in her voice, ignoring that her revelation had silenced the entire room. "Now, I'm going to turn the microphone over to my colleague, William Boyd, who has more tantalizing family histories to present."

William's presentation style was more subdued than Candace, but he shared that the family of Nick Christos, the local handyman, was a founding family, but more interestingly, he had a grandmother who was a World War II spy for the Allies.

By the time we got through Ivy's presentation, we'd learned that the great something-or-other of the guy who owned the local fish stand started one of the first canneries on the coast, and that Mrs. Perez's distant relative arrived in Starry Cove with nothing but his wits and a harmonica.

It was interesting stuff, but nothing to get the room in any type of tizzy. That is until Olivia stepped up to the dais with a secretive smile twitching at the corner of her mouth.

"I am elated," Olivia began, "to present on a woman of great entrepreneurial spirit. A true maverick of her time. An ancestor of your very own Kelly Newman."

"Who?" Trevor asked.

"That's me," Lovie announced with a giggle. "Now hush. I want to hear about this lady. I'm sure she and I have a lot in common."

Olivia raised an eyebrow, then cycled to the next slide. A sturdily built woman with elaborate blonde curls—or what I thought were blonde from a black-and-white photograph—pinned up in her hair smiled out with a toothy grin. She wore frills and laces and satins and sat atop a long bar with bottles lining the back wall. Even in black-and-white, this woman seemed colorful and full of life.

"Maimie Gurtzwald," Olivia said, taking a moment to stare approvingly at the photograph projected on the screen. "Born in Indiana, uneducated, married a Methodist minister, and had three children before the age of twenty." Olivia turned back to the audience. "A typical story of the oppressed women of that era. But Maimie soon grew tired of the drudgery of family life. She stole away on a train headed west, leaving her family behind, and by the age of twenty-three, established herself as the owner of Starry Cove's first saloon and madam of the bawdiest brothel in the west."

***

A stunned silence followed by uproarious howls of laughter filled the community room, drowning out Olivia's voice. A hearty snort erupted from the back through the cackling crowd.

"Be quiet, Shelby," Lovie demanded, stamping her foot. "This isn't funny."

"It's the funniest thing I've ever heard." Shelby wheezed and grabbed a stitch in her side, wiping tears from her cheeks. "Just what did you think you two had in common again?" She erupted into fits, clearly enjoying Lovie's embarrassment, and doubled over as her beehive wobbled with every heave.

Lovie sat down with a huff as Deputy Todd stood up

from beside her. "Settle down," he demanded. "I said, settle down all of you!"

The hubbub subsided, and only a smattering of chuckles still sounded from the audience. Lovie stared straight ahead at the wall with her arms folded while Veronica muttered into her microphone with gusto.

"It may seem humorous now," Olivia said, "but in the late nineteenth century, it was unheard of for a woman to own much of anything outright, let alone run a business by herself. She was a shrewd businesswoman and ultimately divorced her husband—also something unheard of—to marry for love."

"Can we move on?" Deputy Todd urged. It was less a question than a direct order.

Olivia wrinkled her brow and pursed her lips, but shuffled her papers and moved to the next slide. Like the others, it was in black-and-white and foxed on the edges from age. It was also immediately recognizable, as was the figure taking up most of the frame. This had to be the town baker. Portly did not begin to describe the man posing proudly, arms full of bread rolls, with a generous dusting of flour across his apron.

I leaned in close to Angie and whispered, "He looks just like your cousin, Blister. Plus a few pounds."

Angie nodded back with a grin. "And my Grandpa Hauser. This must be mine."

"Starry Cove baker, Bruno Hauser," Olivia said, "emigrated from Germany in 1870 and quickly moved west, bringing his years of baking experience with him. He opened a small but prosperous shop in the middle of town. Before the advent of shopping malls and grocery stores, the bakery provided essential access to food in large quantities that filled the bellies of the thousands of loggers making their way to this region."

Beside me, Angie's feet swung, and she shifted in her seat as if dancing in place.

"It appears the apple hasn't fallen far from the tree, as your local baker, Angie Owens, is a direct descendant of Bruno Hauser."

All eyes shifted toward Angie, who quickly sunk into the chair under their gaze and let her feet lay still. Her cheeks reddened at the attention.

"He was known regionally for his special juniper berry sourdough and, at the time of his death, Bruno claimed he'd used the same sourdough starter passed to him from his father. The recipe remains lost to this day, since no record has ever surfaced documenting Bruno's secretive method." Olivia's eyes skimmed the crowd, but seemed to bore into Angie in passing.

"Juniper berry sourdough," I whispered out of the corner of my mouth to Angie. "Is that even a thing?"

Angie smiled back and whispered through her teeth, "I will make it a thing."

I raised an eyebrow, but my confidence in her baking skills told me she'd succeed.

Julian stepped back up to the dais as Olivia retreated. "That concludes our highlights of the founding families of Starry Cove. We'll now move on to—"

"Ahem." Jim Thornen raised a finger and stood in place.

Julian regarded him with confusion. "Yes?"

"I believe you may have forgotten about my own distinguished ancestry. I have family records that prove my lineage back to the founding of Starry Cove as well."

"And your name?" Julian asked.

"James Thornen III, former multi-term mayor of this town and now raised to county liaison."

"Raised?" Harper scoffed, but Jim ignored her.

Julian riffled through his notes before turning to the group standing behind him with a questioning look. They quickly referred to their notes, flipping pages and scanning names, before Yeardley stepped up to Julian and whispered into his ear. He took a paper from her and gave it a once over. Clearing his throat, he said, "It appears there is record of a Beaufort Thornen present when the town was founded."

Jim twisted to regard the crowd with a satisfied smile spread across his face. "I thought that might be the case."

"Yes," Julian continued, referring to Yeardley's notes. "The records indicate this Beaufort Thornen was a general laborer who, at the time of his death, owed a debt of seventy-five dollars—that's about, oh, two thousand in today's money—to Mr. Claude Goodwin."

Harper's eyes shot our way, and I heard Angie inhale beside me at the recognition of that name. I clutched her wrist to keep her silent. Claude Goodwin. Grandson and heir of the inciter of our treasure hunt, Atticus "Gold Tooth" Goodwin. I wondered how much these genealogists knew about the infamous west coast pirate.

The mention of Claude Goodwin had stunned me enough that I hadn't realized the rest of the room hadn't noticed it at all. Instead, they were more delighted to learn that Jim's ancestor was a destitute nobody than they were at the reference to a strange name. But even Harper, who took every opportunity to deride the former mayor, kept her eyes locked on Angie and me. It was one thing to know of Claude Goodwin ourselves, and another to have the possibility of this group sharing details we thought would remain hidden to time. That we were inviting in this threat hadn't even occurred to me. *But what if they can help us?* Greta's researched had failed to bear fruit despite months of searching. Maybe what we needed was right in front of us, but I tucked the thought away as the presentation continued.

"Now that that's settled, let's move on to the town's newcomers. Equally important, settlers allow towns like Starry Cove to grow from humble beginnings into the communities they are today." Julian ushered Candace back to the podium. "Candace will present first."

From the look on her face, she could hardly contain herself. "This one's a doozy, ladies and gentleman. I am *so* excited to speak on the heritage of your pharmacist, Dr. Ryan MacKenzie."

I shifted a little straighter in my chair. Remembering Candace's hinting, Ryan must have something—or someone—of importance in his history.

"Now, I'm sure you all know that Dr. MacKenzie was born and raised in Scotland." Her eyes twinkled. "And his family has some of the richest Scottish blood, going back generations and generations in the highlands."

I could see little but the back of Ryan's head, so his reaction was hidden from my view. But my nostrils flared as Charlie leaned in to whisper something in his ear, followed by a chuckle from them both.

"But did you know," Candace continued, clicking to the next slide that showed a large stained-glass depiction of what appeared to be an armored knight holding a large sword, "that Dr. MacKenzie is a direct descendant of

William Wallace himself?"

Ryan chortled. "That's something."

Candace waited for a reaction from the rest of the audience, but was met with nothing but blank stares. Her exuberance faded as she realized no one, save a few silent townspeople like me, had any clue about Scottish history.

"Who?" Trevor's face was yet again a mask of confusion.

"William Wallace," Candace repeated as if we hadn't heard. Her eyes scanned the room for any sign of recognition before she let out a heavy sigh. "Braveheart. William Wallace was Braveheart."

That received a more noteworthy reaction from the crowd. Tongues wagged as the room filled with excited murmurs and whispers of "Gibson" and "movie" spread in conversation.

Ryan appeared interested, but humble, conversing with the people directly around him until Candace shushed the crowd so she could go on.

"Wallace was a knight who fought during the Scottish War of Independence and later served as Guardian of Scotland before being drawn and quartered by King Edward I." Candace presented this last tidbit with a vocal flourish. "Truly a fascinating history."

As Candace retreated, Yeardley stepped up to the dais, and we quickly learned that Neil Armstrong was Pastor Basil's third cousin, twice removed, to which Pastor Basil responded with, "Far out, man." And that Shelby Shephard and her beehive were fourth or fifth cousin to Marilyn Monroe. That caused a bit of a stir. Lovie, especially, seemed irritated at that relation.

I leaned in close to Angie and whispered, "I bet

Lovie thought that'd be her story."

Angie nodded and held in a giggle.

Ivy shared that Marty Hardy the mechanic was the eighth great-grandson of the famed Scottish poet Robert Burns. Only Ryan seemed to recognize the name, and let out an endearing "ho ho" as it was announced.

I waited patiently for my turn, wondering what famous relative I'd have hidden away in the recesses of my family tree. A politician? Maybe an explorer or a queen. When Everett stepped up to the podium and announced this was the last presentation before we'd break out into smaller discussion groups, butterflies fluttered in my stomach at the anticipation.

"This is probably you," Angie whispered.

"Stanton Ruttledge," Everett began, "was a man of mysterious origin. Some say he was just another rancher trying to make ends meet in the old west. Others say that Stanton Ruttledge was the alias for none other than 'Dirty Dave' Rudabaugh, an outlaw on the run and onetime associate of Billy the Kid. Rough and filthy, Dirty Dave accounted for the deaths of over ten men, including New Mexico deputies Lino Valdez and James Carlyle."

The audience sat in total silence, not even a breath was heard as we hung on Everett's every word. Outlaws, gunfights—his story had it all as we heard about the life and times of this brutal and violent man.

"It was said that when Dirty Dave escaped from a new Mexico jail, he disappeared into the Pacific northwest, started a family, and lived out his days as a rancher, never speaking about his past. There is no proof, of course, but the rumors persist, and the story has never been disproven. Like many family stories, it is difficult to discern truth from fiction. And so we are left with Stanton Ruttledge, a rancher with no origin, no records, and no history.

"What we do know," Everett continued, "is that Stanton Ruttledge married and had three daughters, and that one of those daughters had a son, and so on and so forth. Which leads us to Starry Cove, where one of you shares a family line with this mysterious man."

People shifted in their seats, but no one said a word. We were all either too scared to learn it was us, or too excited to miss a word Everett had to say. Probably both. Angie squeezed my hand. She must have felt it too.

"It's ironic then," Everett said, "that this outlaw, this maniacal and vicious man, should be the third great-grandfather of Starry Cove Sheriff Deputy Todd Newman."

Lovie recoiled from Deputy Todd's side as he shot up and turned to the crowd. "Hogwash!" he shouted. His oversized hat toppled off his head, and he quickly stuffed it back on. "I don't believe it. Not one word. I'll have you know I come from an upstanding, law-abiding family."

Everett held up his hands as if to wash himself of the matter.

Lovie tugged at his shirt. "Isn't your brother's middle name David?"

"Quiet, Lovie! Grab your things—we're leaving."

Lovie collected her coat and bag and skittered after Deputy Todd, who had already stormed halfway down the aisle toward the door.

Veronica Valentine didn't waste a second, and muttered fervently into her recorder, but the words "outlaw" and "not fit for duty" were said loud enough for all to hear.

As the door slammed behind Deputy Todd and Lovie, I turned to Angie and said, "I guess it wasn't me."

"I wonder if they forgot?"

"Maybe. More likely there's nothing exciting in my family history."

"Everyone's got something, though. Even the fish guy had a story."

"I'll ask during the breakout session, but there's probably nothing worth mentioning. That's my family—bland, boring Lewises."

Eight

JULIAN MADE SHORT closing remarks, then the crowd quickly disbursed into smaller groups with the individual genealogists. I hurried over to catch him before others had a chance to grab his ear.

"Thank you for the wonderful presentation," I said to him.

He shuffled a few papers into a folder. "Thank you, Poppy. We've spent quite a while preparing and we hope these insights will spur people on to investigate more of their pasts."

"I noticed nothing was mentioned about my family. I may have missed the announcements about the breakout groups, and I doubt your group would have forgotten, but I thought I'd check, just in case. Everyone's stories were so interesting."

"Let me check the list." He rustled with his notes again and pulled a sheet from the folder, scanned down a long list of names, then stopped and said, "Looks like you were one of Randall's." He shook his head and tsked.

"Tragic, that. You'll want to talk to Everett, though. He took over all of Randall's work and could tell you if there was anything to share."

I thanked him as a crowd grew around us. Everyone was eager to learn about their families. Everett, too, had a group waiting for his attention. As I approached, he and Olivia were in the midst of a heated, but polite, conversation.

"The fact remains," Everett was saying, "there are more detailed histories of the male lines because that is where the history lay." His words were clear and emotionless, unlike Olivia, who seemed ready to pop.

"The only reason their history is what is considered history is because they wrote the history." Olivia emoted wildly with her arms and hands. "If women were given even the slightest opportunity to write their own history, it would be just as much, if not more, interesting than any man's story."

"We will have to agree to disagree then."

"I don't agree to anything," Olivia retorted. "Just like a man to shut a woman down."

Everett turned away, ignoring the rest of her words, leaving her to seethe and turn to her own group. After a few deep breaths, she seemed to calm down, and greeted them warmly one by one.

Everett's face had not changed. He seemed to wear the same stoic face whether he was eating breakfast or fighting with Olivia.

I waited patiently as the others learned about their families. These tidbits were less interesting than outlaws and madams, but Mrs. Hallerman seemed just as riveted to learn that her great-great-grandfather was a mason as

Mr. Tran was to find out that his mother's grandfather immigrated to America in 1903 and survived the devastating San Francisco earthquake.

I waited patiently for the rest to finish, soaking in the words along with them, until everyone finished and Everett was left alone.

"Julian told me you may have Randall's notes about my family."

He regarded me coolly, as if he were doing me a grand favor, but referred to the notes in his file. "If I have anything it would be listed here, but I don't see that Randall's notes mention your past at all. Are you sure you submitted a request?"

"Yes," I said. "Same as the others."

"Then I'm sorry." Everett closed his folder. "Randall's notes were sparse to begin with, so he may have had something memorized, although that's unlikely."

I let out a small sigh. Disappointed, for sure, but tried to remind myself that I could have been tied to a long line of manure wranglers or some dodgy criminal element and it was better to have no knowledge than learn an unfortunate fact.

Everett must have noticed my disappointment. "I can look into it for you, if you'd like? It won't be anything comprehensive, but I'm sure I can turn over something of value."

"No," I said. "No, it's fine. I'm sure you're busy."

Everett hoisted his folder under his arm, a hint that his part of our conversation was over. "Perhaps more of Randall's notes will turn up."

"Thanks anyway," I said with a smile, and turned to find Angie waiting beside me.

"No luck, huh?"

"Nothing. Randall was responsible for my information, so he either didn't do it, or it's lost."

"Too bad," Angie said.

"What's too bad?" Harper slinked beside us, Dewey drooping in her arms.

"There's nothing about Poppy's family."

"Bummer. Looks like you have to live in blissful ignorance like me."

"You should have put your name in," Angie said to her. "Who knows what they could have found out about your family."

Harper set Mayor Dewey onto a nearby chair and he curled up on the spot. It was probably still warm from someone's bottom, and definitely warmer than the floor.

"I appreciate you nosing into my business, Angie, but no thanks. Besides, we have more important things to discuss, anyway."

"Like what?" Angie asked.

"Like how Jim Thornen's a pathetic loser."

"Or," I said more firmly, "how there are apparently records out there about Claude Goodwin."

"Oh, yeah," said Angie. "That was surprising."

"That means my guests may know more about him."

Angie tapped her chin. "Right… Should we ask them, though? I thought we'd want to keep it, you know, a secret." Her eyes darted left and right, making sure no one overheard.

"Yeah," Harper said. "I don't know about blabbing to these folks. We don't even know who we can trust. Remember Cho?"

I had not forgotten Cho, nor how we'd been burned

before by trusting blindly. "You're right. This might not be the best time. But maybe we can dig for information without coming right out and asking."

"I'll let you work that out," said Harper. "I'm only good at blunt demands."

"There's something else," I said. "During breakfast this morning, my guests mentioned church records, but also old records that may be kept here."

"Here?" Harper glanced around, disbelieving.

"Is there an attic or basement or anything?"

Harper frowned. "I know all the doors in this building. There's no basement."

"What about an attic?" Angie asked. "There's got to be some type of storage space."

Harper shrugged. "We can look." She peered around at the large crowd still milling in the main meeting room. "But now isn't the best time."

"Tomorrow?" I asked.

Harper nodded. "After my mail route. Let's say ten o'clock. How about you, Angie?"

Angie stared at Harper dead-eyed. "Ten o'clock?" she repeated, incredulous. "How is that a real job?"

Harper shrugged. "I can't help it if I'm efficient."

The little woman let out a reluctant sigh. "I guess Cesar can watch the bakery for a while. What about the stuff at the church?"

"That'll have to wait. I can't imagine Pastor Basil saying no to anyone, but he's probably only got old marriage and death records. Town Hall will have all the interesting documents. If we can find out anything about Claude Goodwin's business dealings, it could help us figure out where he may have hidden the rest of his grandfather's treasure."

"Okay, then," Harper said with a firm nod. "Tomorrow it is."

"Good," I said. "We'll meet here at ten. I want first crack at those records before anyone else."

* * *

Everyone had settled in that evening back at the Pearl while I recounted the night's events to Greta as we washed up in the kitchen. Mayor Dewey, who followed me home from the town meeting, sat patiently on a small table against the wall, washing his paws in silent routine.

"Sounds like a load of baloney," Greta announced from atop her wooden stool in front of the sink.

"It was actually quite fascinating, hearing about everyone's families."

She only grunted in response.

I eyed her sideways. "What about your family?"

Greta paused for a moment, hands still submerged in the soapy water, then continued washing. "Nothing to tell."

I frowned. Angie and I had pushed it with Harper earlier, but Greta was unpredictable, so I let the matter go. She clearly didn't want to share—at least not with me, so I opted to change the subject. "We're going to the community center tomorrow to sniff out the old town records Everett mentioned at breakfast."

Greta gave me an agitated look. "Why'd you send me all the way to the county library then?"

"The library is important, too."

"Pah," she said, waving a soapy hand. "Don't know why I'm complaining."

"I'll need you at the community center tomorrow, though."

She stared at me with her mouth agape, but as she started to say something, she nearly tumbled off her stool.

I grabbed her arm and steadied her before she fell. "Are you all right?" I asked. "What's wrong?"

"I was going to the library tomorrow. My research…"

"That can wait. Obviously, the town records are more important."

Greta pursed her lips as she dried her hands on a grimy towel and stepped down from the stool. "I was just on the cusp of a new discovery."

"Were you now?" I asked dryly.

"Well, I was due to make a discovery, at least. Any time now."

"You just want to ride that scooter, don't you?"

Greta scoffed and stuck her hairy chin in the air. "I wish to dwell in the house of knowledge."

"*House of knowledge*. Who do you think you're kidding?" I raised an eyebrow, and she yielded with a slump of her shoulders. "We'll head to the community center after washing up from breakfast tomorrow."

"Suit yourself." She huffed once and turned away, no doubt headed to the library off the foyer.

I grabbed a fresh mug of coffee and scooped Mayor Dewey off the table with my free arm. Kicking the screen door open, I maneuvered onto the porch. The night was cold and crisp, and the steam from my coffee billowed up and filled my nostrils. I closed my eyes and inhaled deeply. Delicious.

"A bit late for coffee, isn't it?"

My eyes popped open. Candace sat on a bench next to Yeardley, and both were bundled in puffy coats and fuzzy scarves.

"It's never too late," I said, smiling. "Mind if I have a seat?"

"Course not." She let out a weak laugh. "It's your house, isn't it?"

A slight tilt to my head acknowledged the fact as I sat down. Dewey crawled from my arms and curled up on the bench beside me.

"Well, I'm off to begin my nightly routine." Candace stood up and patted her cheeks. "When you get to be my age, nothing works right. You've got to wrangle every-thing into place with creams and serums. Never get old, Poppy. It's too dang expensive."

Yeardley, who hadn't shared a word, simply watched as Candace retreated inside. She also held a warm mug of steamy coffee. Catching my glance, she said, "Candace gives me a hard time for my late-night caffeine, too. But I don't pay her any mind." She clutched the mug tighter. "It's like a security blanket."

I knew exactly what she meant, and held mine closer, too.

Yeardley nodded toward Dewey. "I had a cat that looked like him once. A big orange guy, except mine was rough around the edges, you know? Missing bits out of one ear and his whiskers were always bent like he'd just woken up after a hard night out."

I ran a gentle hand along Dewey's fur. "This guy is so spoiled."

"You can never spoil them enough, though, right? I'm so fascinated that he's the mayor. There was a man tonight… Thornen, I think his name was.”

I nodded. “He used to be mayor before Dewey.”

“He was beaten by a cat?”

I nodded again and chuckled. “I’m not sure if you caught on, but Jim Thornen is a pain in the you-know-what.”

“He seems like a tall glass of trouble.”

“More like a sharp pebble in the bottom of your shoe,” I said. “Anyway, it was such an interesting presentation tonight. You all must have worked very hard.”

“We prepare as best we can. Sometimes, like in Mr. Thornen’s case, we don’t have much to share. People just, you know, got on with life back then. Nothing special, just life.”

“There must be a lot of interesting stories, though. I heard Randall talking about his manuscript. Do you know if he was writing about Starry Cove?”

At the mention of Randall, Yeardley’s eyes dropped to her coffee.

“Oh,” I said. “I’m sorry. That was insensitive of me.”

“No, no. It’s all right. He was working on a manuscript, but I’m not sure if it was about your town.”

“And what about you?” I asked gingerly, remembering Julian’s words and the notebook she’d hidden earlier.

“Me?”

I nodded. “Was that what you were hiding earlier? Are you working on something, too? You don’t have to be shy about it.”

“I… Maybe.” She nodded and shook her head as if unsure of her answer. “Yes, I am working on something.” She bit her lip and quickly added, “But it’s not fit for anyone’s eyes yet.”

"I'm sure it will be wonderful."

"Probably not as magnificent as Randall's would have been."

"Nonsense," I said. "You're a researcher too, right?"

She nodded. "Yes, but Randall was meticulous. His notes were…"

"Were what?"

She shook her head as if she couldn't find the words and tears sprang in her eyes.

"Were you two friends?"

Yeardley didn't answer.

"You stood up for him at breakfast, so I thought maybe…"

"No, but… I guess…" She struggled to speak. "Randall puts everyone down. Or did. But now he's dead. It's just a lot to process."

I nodded, sympathizing with her grief. "Seems like Randall may have been insecure."

Yeardley laughed with a snide guffaw. "That's one word for it. He was the worst around Everett and Olivia, though."

"Why them?"

Yeardley turned her watery eyes to me. "Because he knew they were smarter than him. It ate at him, everyone could tell. Everett's very intelligent—he's got two PhDs and everything. A *real* historian, not like me…"

"There you go again," I said, "putting yourself down."

She continued with a slight shake of her head. "Everett's the newest of our group—just a few months—and not long after he joined, he corrected Randall on a primary source and it was a whole big blowup. After that,

Randall questioned all of Everett's research, down to the smallest thing."

"And here I was thinking William and Randall were the problem."

Yeardley rolled her eyes. "Oh, that, too."

"Sounds like Randall didn't get along with anyone, but I heard at breakfast that he shared his notes with Everett. That seems odd, considering what you just said."

"Knowing Randall, it was probably an attempt to show off. Drone on to Everett about all he knew. Show him up, that sort of thing. It's a good thing he did, though." She grew quiet again. "But I don't think anyone expected this. It's hard to put it out of your mind."

"Perhaps," I said, collecting Dewey and standing up, "what we both need is a good night's sleep."

We shuffled inside through the front door, and as Yeardley plodded upstairs and I turned the lights out for the evening, I couldn't help but wonder if Randall's nagging led someone to do the unthinkable. And, like Yeardley had said, it was hard to put it out of my mind as I lay awake that night.

Nine

GRETA CORNERED ME the following morning while preparing breakfast. I hadn't slept well and was suffering from a serious lack of coffee, so I wasn't at my best, and she took full advantage of the moment.

"Can I ride the scooter?"

"It's only three hundred yards to the community center, Greta."

"So?"

"We can walk there faster than you can put on your gear and ride there."

"Irrelevant to my question."

I finally waved her off so I could reach the coffee maker. "Fine, whatever. You can ride it, but I expect you to really help with digging through those files."

Greta cackled softly and rubbed her hands together. She really was a persistent little troll sometimes, but as long as she stuck to the rules we'd established, I couldn't find a good reason to say no.

"Let's get breakfast on the table," I said. "You can

daydream about the scooter later."

Today's morning meal consisted of individual servings of what Greta called a hootenanny, but I remembered them called Dutch babies, which I found disturbing in its own way, but delicious if I avoid imagining myself feasting on European infants.

The group waited in the common room until they saw Greta and me swivel through the dining room door. Chattering floated my way, but died down as they took their seats at the table.

"Thank you both for this lovely meal," Julian said. "We've certainly appreciated your hospitality, all things considered."

"It's no problem at all," I replied. "I hope everyone slept well."

"Like a baby," Olivia said. "Why's your face all scrunched up, Ivy? What's on your mind."

"Me?" Ivy had been rubbing her shoulder, but suddenly stopped, seeming surprised at the question. "I'm okay, it's just my arm has been hurting a lot."

"Probably sleeping on it wrong," said Candace. "I had that problem once when I dislocated my arm. They had to pop it right back in." She mimed popping her arm back into its socket. "I thought that hurt, but then I slept on it wrong and learned my mistake real quick."

"Maybe," Ivy said just as the door rang.

I left Greta to finish serving, and as I reached the door, I made out the bulbous shape of Deputy Todd's hat in the sidelights. Mayor Dewey idled on the porch railing and only blinked, but made no move, as I opened the front door.

"Good morning, deputy."

He tipped his ridiculous hat. "Good morning, Miss Lewis," The twangy drawl of his voice held no good news. "I'm here to—"

"Deputy!" came a shout from the street. "Deputy, I demand to speak with you."

I peered around Deputy Todd to see Jim Thornen marching up the walkway in strides as long as his tight jeans and cowboy boots would allow.

"What is it now, Jim? Did someone accidentally step on your lawn again?"

Jim bristled. "I'll have you know my rights have been violated."

"Is that so?"

"That *is* so. I have requested use of the community center for my Founders Club meeting and was just denied for absolutely no reason."

"What's a Founders Club meeting?" I asked.

Jim ran his gaze over me once as if deciding if I could exist on my own porch, then sniffed. "It's a meeting for Starry Cove founding families, if you must know. A place for historical discussion and heartfelt remembrance of those who have come before." He turned to face Deputy Todd. "And Harper Tillman had the audacity to say I could only use the community center if the *mayor* allowed it."

Our eyes swiveled to Mayor Dewey, who blinked lazily from the railing in the morning fog.

"I know my rights, deputy. And the bylaws state I can request access to use the community center during certain hours and Harper has no reason to refuse. I demand she be arrested."

"Arrested?" I scoffed. "For what?"

"For refusing my rightful request."

Deputy Todd let out a deep sigh and rocked back on the heels of his boots.

"As you just stated," I said, "Harper has no authority and you'll have to work it out with the mayor."

"The *mayor*," Jim spat.

"That's right, the mayor," Deputy Todd said flatly. "Well?"

Jim huffed and crossed his arms. I'm sure he seethed inside at the internal struggle between obtaining use of the community center and maintaining his silly pride. Finally, he turned to Dewey and gritted his teeth. "May I use the community center?" The question came out in pointed syllables, each word a struggle.

The deputy rolled his exasperated eyes Dewey's way, and the cat blinked once. "See?" Deputy Todd affirmed, rolling his eyes back to Jim. "I take that as a yes. No problem here, right Jim?"

"The problem," Jim sputtered, "is that this town is an absolute mockery." Then he turned heel and stomped down the walkway the way he'd come, leaving us standing on the porch in the chilly morning air.

"As I was saying," Deputy Todd started, "I was hoping to talk to your guests. The autopsy results are in for Randall Portsmouth."

"That was fast," I said.

"Well, pardon me," he drawled sarcastically. "Apparently the coroner is pretty bored most of the time. You seem to be the source of all suspicious deaths in the county, Miss Lewis."

Ouch. I winced at that one. "And?" I asked.

"And what, Miss Lewis?"

"What were the results?"

"I told you before, I don't share with civilians."

"Just tell me, please," I urged. "Is Angie in trouble?"

Deputy Todd considered this a moment, then said in a low voice, "Not choking, but also not a heart attack."

"What then?"

"That's what toxicology will tell us. Which," he said trying to look past me, "is why I need to talk to your guests. I need them to stay in town for the time being, at least until the tox results come back."

"How long will that be?"

He held up his hands. "No idea, but I'm sure you can accommodate for a few more days. Or is the inn all booked up for the winter?" His grin told me he knew I had no other reservations, so I sighed and let him pass over the threshold.

***

"I cannot believe the nerve of that guy." Harper paced the community center floor, repeating ad nauseam how much of a fool and a pain Jim Thornen was to her. She threw up her hands once again. "*Founders Club*! What a stupid idea. I hope you're not thinking of joining, Angie."

"Of course not. Don't be silly."

I shared a tired look with Angie and steadied the ladder below the opening we'd found that led to the attic. It was just large enough for one of us to fit through. Harper was too tall and lanky, and too uncoordinated to be the obvious choice. Angie, short and stout and covered in flour, would also not do, and neither she nor Greta could reach the attic perch from even the topmost rung of the ladder. Which left me to brave the dusty cobwebs in order to pass down anything of interest I may find.

"Look on the bright side," Angie said to Harper. "Maybe now Jim won't have time to get involved with, um, that other meeting."

"SCAT," Harper said. "It's not a bad word, Angie."

"I know." Angie cast her eyes downward and picked at the strings on her apron. "It just sounds like one."

Greta grunted nearby. "Sounds like a load of poop to me." She still wore her helmet from the short ride down the road, and loose strands of her long gray hair stuck out haphazardly through the straps.

Harper ignored Greta and focused on Angie and me. "And did you see Veronica Valentine's article this morning? The usual trash."

"Do you have it?" Angie asked. "Let me see."

Harper pulled a crinkled copy of the *Vista View* from her mail bag. She'd come straight to the community center after her route, like she said she would, and still wore the distinctive uniform, but accented with her usual rainbow accessories. Today was a long multi-colored scarf, wound around her neck a few times before the ends disappeared into her coat.

I hadn't read the article either, as my guests, eager to read Veronica's take on their presentation, took turns passing the paper between them, leaving me no chance at a look myself.

Angie read off the headline, "Ancestry Scandal Too Much to Handle." She looked up from the paper with a worried face. "That doesn't sound good."

"Read on," Harper said, waving a hand. "She really took it to Deputy Todd, and I only feel a smidge bad for Lovie now that the whole county knows her grandma was a—"

"Listen to this!" Angie cleared her throat and read aloud, "Angela Owens, winner of this year's Pie Parade, will surely feel at home in her bakery after learning that her ancestor, Bruno Hauser, was an elite baker in his own right." Angie looked up at us in wonderment. "She didn't say anything mean. Not about my bakery, and there's absolutely nothing about cinnamon rolls."

"Looks like Lovie's and Todd's scandals outweighed yours," Harper said.

"Shoot," I said, shaking my head. "I forgot to tell you guys."

"What?" Harper and Angie asked in unison.

"Deputy Todd came by this morning. And I'll bet from that article that Veronica already knows, too."

"What?" they repeated, more urgently this time.

"That Randall Portsmouth didn't choke on Angie's cinnamon roll."

"He didn't?" Angie's face lit up. "That's great news. Er, I mean," she looked around sheepishly, "it's terrible that he's dead, of course."

"He didn't have a heart attack either, and now we're waiting on the toxicology report."

"Toxicology?" Harper wondered. "Poison?"

"Possibly," I said, shrugging.

"Oh, no," Angie wailed. "That won't help me at all. People will still think I poisoned him."

"People will think whatever they want to think."

"Poppy's right," Greta piped in. "People think I'm a kooky oddball, can you believe that? Well," she said, crossing her arms defiantly, "we know better, don't we?"

Angie's face melted into a puddle of worry. Greta's

attempt to soften the blow only exacerbated it. Maybe bringing her along wasn't the best idea. "Why don't we get started? All this speculation isn't helping."

I fought the cobwebs and dust, and found the election box and some other interesting Starry Cove artifacts before wading into a sea of banker boxes filled with loosely filed paperwork. One glance inside the first box with my flashlight and I knew these might be the old records we were searching for. Faded and ink-stained newspaper clippings were packed along with hand-written logs with official looking seals and a number of sealed envelopes. Who knew what those held? Wills? Deeds?

I shouted down to the others, "It's a time capsule up here. I'm going to pass down boxes."

Soon enough, the pile of records were hauled down the ladder and the four of us sat in folding chairs in front of folding tables, unfolding decaying pieces of paper—maybe papyrus by the age and look of some of them.

"What exactly are we looking for?" Angie asked.

"We'll know when we see it," I said. "But basically anything that might have to do with Claude Goodwin or excavations or that type of thing."

We searched silently for a long while with no success until Angie held up a dank envelope with her thumb and forefinger. An unidentifiable brown stain marred one corner. "Wouldn't the people at your bed-and-breakfast be better at sifting through this stuff?"

"Pah," Greta scoffed and blew a billowy cloud of dust off an uneven stack of papers. "I've got more research—"

Harper interrupted. "Yes, yes we know. You've got more skills in your big toe or little finger or gigantic derriere or whatever." She slapped a cracked leather ledger down on the table. "It's just a bunch of moldy books and stuff. I'm tired of moldy books and notebooks and old furniture, Poppy. Where's the gold?"

"Gold? That sounds like fun."

Harper, Angie and I swiveled to find two silhouettes backlit against the wide opening of the community center doors. The small amount of light filtering through the fog gave the taller figure a halo of copper hair—Candace. A gently cradled arm indicated the other was Ivy. Greta, who ignored the intrusion, hummed lightly to herself and continued turning pages.

"Hello," I said in a manner I hoped sounded casual. "Is there something wrong at the house?"

"No, nothing like that," she said. "Just thought we'd take a stroll, and we saw that scooter of yours laying on the grass out front."

I shot a glare at Greta, who continued to hum as if she hadn't heard. "We'll talk later," I hissed, then turned back to Candace. "Thanks, everything is fine, though."

"Glad to hear it. What are you all up to?" She raised on her tip toes to get a look at the table. Ivy, meek and shy, remained by the door.

"We're just, uh…"

"Organizing some files," Harper said at the same time I said, "Cleaning the attic."

Harper and I glanced at one another and frowned.

"We're organizing the files that were in the attic," I said. "I remembered Everett mentioned wanting to take a look and thought we'd get a head start."

"Splendid," Candace boomed in the near-empty room. "I bet we'd all like to get our hands on all those little nuggets of history." She twiddled her fingers eagerly. "Makes my heart flutter at the thought. The church, too. All those family bibles and marriage records."

"Is the church really as old as Julian claimed?" Angie asked.

"You'll just have to show up tonight and find out, won't you?" Candace let a sly smile escape at the side of her mouth.

"What was Everett hoping to find here?" I indicated the piles of paper on the table.

"Something Randall wanted, no doubt."

"What does that mean?" I asked.

"Their rivalry." This time it was Ivy who spoke up. "It was terrible."

"What she means is, Everett and Randall didn't always see eye to eye."

"Yeardley told me about their fight."

"Fight?" Candace mused. "Yes, you could call it that. Bit of a doozy, too. Those men, terrible communicators." She flicked a hand as if dismissing it away as a simple fact. "Everett likes to think he's some type of smooth talker. He's rich or something, dresses nice and all, but he just comes off as slippery, right Ivy?"

Ivy nodded reluctantly then bit her lip as if she'd said too much, when she'd said nothing at all.

Candace continued, "He probably thinks I'm a tough nut."

"Which one?" Harper asked.

"Both of them, but I wouldn't give Randall a minute of my time. Did you know he was angling to take over leadership of our group?" Candace scoffed.

"To take over for Julian?" I couldn't imagine Randall

would be a better leader than Julian, who was kind and levelheaded.

Ivy nodded again. "He said the group could use a more distinguished leader. Someone who would give us the status we deserved."

"Status," Candace repeated as if it were a vice. "He was the only one concerned with status, but he was too thick-headed to see it."

My eyes flickered to Ivy, who I remembered seemed uncomfortable talking about a dead man. "Well," I said softly, "no matter now."

"Right you are," Candace said. "Ivy, shall we carry on to the church and see what we're up against tonight." She turned to the three of us sitting at the table and winked.

They disappeared into the fog and I turned back to my friends. "If Randall was trying to take over the group, do you think Julian could have done something to prevent it?"

"You heard what she said, though," Angie said, shaking her head. "There was no way she would have chosen Randall over Julian. Wouldn't Julian have a good sense of their feelings toward Randall?"

I nodded. I also thought Julian would know better, but I couldn't put it to rest that easily. "Probably, but I'm interested to hear what he has to say on the matter."

"Are we done here?" Harper droned. "It looks like someone's office threw up on the table."

"I'd say so." Greta hopped off her chair. "You all should get this packed up."

"Us?" Harper snapped.

"I've got to get back to turn down the rooms." Greta

waddled toward the door without looking back, still humming that insufferable tune, leaving the three of us to clean up the mess.

***

The door chime at the diner belied my dour mood. With nothing to show for our efforts at the community center, I left to get lunch at Shelby's down the street.

Jim's Founders Club, it seemed, was the talk of the town, and as I entered, I could tell everyone had an opinion.

"No ancestry of note so he's got to rustle up some importance." Shelby filled coffee mugs down the line at the counter, but didn't stop talking. "Doesn't get to run the town anymore, so he's got to puff himself up like a bulldog. Hey there, dearie, you want a seat?" Shelby motioned for me to take an empty spot at the counter.

"Talking about Jim, I take it?"

"Even Mason's strutting around with his pimply beak in the air knowing his family goes all the way back. Lovie, too. Why, she couldn't jump fast enough at the chance to join Jim's exclusive little club."

"I'm surprised at some of the names from last night. Even Nick is a founder. I didn't expect that." Nick Christos was the best-looking man in the town, maybe even the county. I'd assumed his family emigrated from Greece, or wherever Greek gods came from, more recently than not.

Shelby leaned in to avoid being overheard. "Nick, dearie, couldn't *founder* his way out a plastic doggy bag." She tsked once. "Bless his gorgeous heart."

The bell chimed behind me as Ursula and Ryan

arrived, doffing their winter coats.

"Lunch'll be up in a second, dearies."

I tried not to make eye contact, still sore and disappointed from my conversation with Ryan the other day.

Ursula had other ideas. "Hello there, Poppy. You here for lunch, too?"

"Mm-hmm," I mumbled, feigning intense interest in the menu board on the wall.

"I suppose you've heard of Jim's Founders Club, then?"

"Yep. He came by the house earlier."

"He didn't even bother to come into the General Store. I guess he figured he didn't need to since Dr. MacKenzie and I aren't founders." She said the last word with disgust.

"He asked Angie to join the club," I said, "but she declined."

"Good for her," Ursula said. "Glad she's got the common sense to see through Jim's divisive tactics."

"Jim's a big ninny, dearie. Nothing but a ninny."

Ryan hadn't offered much to the conversation. Being the perfect gentleman he usually is, no doubt. Kind of got under your skin after a while. Why'd he have to be such a nice guy? What's he thinking? Why did he choose a green sweater today? Was it because green was my favorite—

"Poppy?"

I blinked twice, then shook myself out of it. "Sorry, what?"

"I was saying," Ursula repeated, "that Georgia came into the shop this morning looking awfully proud, as if my store was her birthright."

Shelby sniffed. "Scandalous, dearies."

"And she didn't even buy anything. Anyway, it was Trevor who told us about the club. He joined, of course. Said he wants to learn more about the *tonsorial arts*."

Ursula continued to drone on at Shelby's receptive nods. Ryan stepped closer to where I sat at the counter.

"You seem to be avoiding me," he said.

"I thought that's what you wanted." That thought was supposed to stay in my head, but the words fell out from sheer surprise. *I'd* been avoiding *him*? "I mean, I thought you wanted me to back off because of your son. Is he with you?"

"He's in school right now. Or at least I hope he is and the administration office hasn't called me yet today."

An awkward silence followed before I said, "I've got the Vespa going."

"Aye, I've seen it around, although it wasn't you steering it, unless you've shrunk and all your hair's gone gray."

I cringed a little on the inside. "That's my housekeeper."

"And how is the grand opening going?"

"Besides my dead guest?"

He winced. "Sorry, forgot about that bit. How are you doing, then?"

"As well as can be expected, I think."

"Aye. It had to be a fairly traumatic experience."

"He… He fell into my arms. Then he just, you know, died. He was so clammy." I shivered at the memory. "And his eyes were… nothing but blue. That's what I remember, at least."

"Clammy, you say?"

"Yeah, he was sweating like he'd just run a marathon."

"And his eyes had no pupils?"

I turned to face Ryan directly. "Do you know something?"

He stared thoughtfully at the ground. I could tell there was something on his mind. "I'm not sure," he said finally, "but it sounds like he was having a reaction."

"A reaction?"

"Possibly to something in his system. Do you remember anything else?"

Those seconds were mostly a blur in my memory and only a few elements stood out like Randall's clammy hands, his sweaty face, those eyes, and... "He came down the stairs like he was drunk. Stumbling, you know?"

"Stumbling." Ryan nodded once as if confirming his suspicions.

"What is it?"

Ryan leaned closer so none could hear, close enough that I could smell his aftershave. My cheek grazed his, and I felt his warm breath as he whispered in my ear, "I suspect your guest died of an overdose."

I jerked back, shocked, mouthing the word without sound. Keeping my voice low, I asked, "Would that show on a toxicology report?"

He nodded. "Aye. We see it a lot in my line of work—addiction, overdoses, that sort of thing."

I let this sink in. I didn't know Randall from a biscuit, but he didn't come across as anyone with a substance abuse problem. Then again, if Randall overdosed, that would clear up any lingering suspicion surrounding Angie's cinnamon rolls.

Shelby's voice broke up my thoughts. "Look here, dearies, I'm not going to take this laying down. We need to mount a proper response."

"Response?" I asked.

"To Jim's Founders Club. He's gone completely bonkers."

"Mm-hmm," was all I could muster. Shelby must have taken that as agreement, as she nodded and shifted to a more detailed exchange with Ursula.

"That sounds like trouble," Ryan whispered.

A ding from the kitchen announced Ursula's and Ryan's to-go orders were ready, and Shelby disappeared into the kitchen. As she exited, the front door chimed open and Cesar popped his head in, searched the room, finally landed on me before smiling and continuing inside.

"Hello Poppy. Angie told me you might be here."

Cesar maneuvered his way to the counter next to me and Ryan stepped back a few feet and frowned.

"Hi Cesar, what's up?"

"Thought I'd pop over and grab a bite, too." He swiveled into the seat by my side, pushing Ryan further away.

Shelby arrived and handed Ryan his packed lunch. She spotted Cesar at the chair next to me and raised an eyebrow.

I wanted to say more to Ryan before he left, but reminded myself that he wanted his space, so I said nothing. He and Ursula quickly disappeared through the door into the cold air, headed back to the General Store. When Shelby and her beehive wandered over to take my order, I couldn't help but notice a twinge of a frown at the corner of her mouth as she glanced at Cesar sitting by my side.

***

Greta insisted the rooms had all been serviced when I arrived back after lunch. I was grateful she'd taken it all on without my help, but skeptical that she hadn't cut corners to complete the job as fast as she claimed. In her eagerness to get to the library—back onto the scooter, really—she accosted me on the porch, hopping from foot to foot as she does when I know she's excited.

"All the rooms?" I asked again.

"All of them," she confirmed.

"And what about what Candace said? Earlier, about the scooter parked on the lawn."

"A simple precaution."

I blinked. "A precaution against what?"

"Scratching the paint."

I was used to Greta's roundabout excuses, but they were still exasperating. I let out a heavy sigh. "You parked on the community center lawn at ten in the morning to avoid getting paint scratches? From what?"

"Ruffians."

"Ruffians," I repeated. "There are a lot of ruffians in Starry Cove, are there?"

"I thought you'd appreciate that I was taking good care of the scooter."

"No more parking on the lawn. Park in the designated spots, like everyone else."

"Suit yourself," she said with a huff. "But don't be surprised if your scooter comes back covered in scratches and dings."

My shoulders sagged. She was exhausting sometimes. "Just do your best."

Now, as she zoomed toward the Vista library, I peeked into the ground-floor rooms before heading upstairs to confirm Greta's work for myself. A few guests lingered in the common room and I'd spotted Julian in the library off the foyer as I entered the house. I'd expected most of them to fill their time waiting on the toxicology report by engaging in scholarly pursuits or some other stodgy activity, but Olivia and Yeardley were engrossed in a lively board game and William, ensconced in a large cushioned chair, worked intently on the sudoku puzzle from today's *Vista View*.

Upstairs, the beds should all be made, the dishes cleared, and fresh water laid out on the serving tray in each room. I had one hand on the knob for Ivy's room, when I noticed the door to the Victorian suite was ajar. I moved with silent footsteps across the landing and peered through the slit between the door and the frame.

A figure moved in and out of my field of vision, traversing the room. They must be stepping lightly because I heard no footsteps from within. On the large Victorian bed sat a box of jumbled items—mostly papers and folders. Randall's belongings.

Without warning, I burst into the room. "Just what do you think you are doing?" I asked sternly.

The figure, now at the bedside, turned around. Everett, his hair slicked into a perfect coif, regarded me without expression. "May I help you?" he asked.

"May I help *you*?"

He laid a hand on the box. "I had follow-up questions from the residents and I needed to refer to Randall's notes." He let out a soft sigh, "Still nothing about you, I'm afraid."

I flushed, feeling foolish having barged in.

"The furniture in here is exquisite. Julian's description did not do it justice."

"Thank you," I said. "It was part of my inheritance."

"Ah, yes." He strolled to the armoire and ran an appreciative hand down its side.

"Did you find what you were looking for?"

His eyes went back to the box. "Yes, mostly. I'm not sure what the others have told you, but Randall and I were not always of the same mind."

"So I've heard."

He nodded knowingly. "There was tension. Randall's pride was legendary."

"Then why would he share his research with you? Why not one of the others? Candace, perhaps."

"Candace?" Everett sneered. "Not likely Candace."

"Why not?"

"I'm quite certain Candace hated Randall, and the feeling was mutual. She's just like him, you see. She admitted she'd never forgive him, never apologize. I'm surprised she didn't burst into fits of laughter as he tumbled down the stairs and lay dying."

Based on my own conversations with Candace, Everett probably wasn't far off the truth. "So why you then?"

"Because, unlike Candace, Randall and I could set aside our differences. There is a respect between gentlemen that the others wouldn't understand."

Everett was so calm and formal in his manner. I felt silly having burst in making accusations like a squawking chicken.

"If you think I harmed Randall, then you're wrong,"

he said. "But if you're considering the others, it's William you want to look out for."

"And why's that?"

"Candace was one thing, but William and Randall feuded like the infamous Hatfields and McCoys—endless quarrels dragged through every speck of their existence."

"Julian warned me about them."

Everett moved closer and his voice took a serious tone. "William's entire persona is a farce. The leather vest, the motorcycle—all bravado with no substance. Even his biker gang is a figment of his imagination, and Randall reminded William every chance he got. Perhaps William grew tired of Randall's constant belittlement? He has terribly thin skin, you know. And if I remember correctly, he slipped away from the larger group not long before Randall tumbled down the stairs. I'd say that's suspicious, wouldn't you?"

My lip twisted as I considered this. But none of this explained why Randall clearly pointed at Olivia as he died. "What about Olivia?" I asked. "Randall practically accused her with his dying breath."

Everett's mouth curled up at the corners into a condescending smile. "Olivia wouldn't have what it takes. She's too… messy."

"Messy?"

"She's outspoken and brash—claws her way up trees she has no business in. Now, if you'll excuse me?" He gave the room one last admiring look before striding past me and through the door.

I felt the wave of embarrassment wash over me again as I stepped aside. Some host I was, berating my own guests. Of course Everett was in here—I'd almost asked him myself to recheck Randall's papers, and now it seemed obvious that other residents would have had questions, too.

I leaned against the bed, disappointed in myself, and let my eyes roam the room. Nothing appeared out of place. But why would it? A faint voice inside my head answered: because Everett wasn't just looking at Randall's notes—he was wandering around the room when I peeked in. Admiring the furniture, perhaps. My eyes narrowed. Or perhaps something else.

Ten

THE EVENING WAS cold and the crispness bit at you with every whip of the wind off the water. Angie and Harper walked with me along the sidewalk from the bakery, where we'd convened, to the non-denominational Fellowship of the Faith church just a few hundred yards down Main Street. Harper carried Mayor Dewey in her arms like a sack of potatoes.

"Oof," Harper said with a grunt, "this guy's getting heavy. No more treats, man."

"You're aware he can walk, right?"

Harper shot me a scandalized look. "It's winter, Poppy. His little paws will freeze."

"Maybe he's so large because he never gets to walk himself anymore. You carry him around like a giant furry baby."

"Are you all right, Poppy?" Angie's voice held a note of concern. "You're awfully snippy tonight."

I caught myself before I could snip a reply. "Sorry," I said finally. "Greta got home from the library after dark.

I always get nervous when she's out after dark, and my nerves are probably still on edge."

"Why was she out so late?" Harper asked.

"Apparently, she thought she'd stop and forage for mushrooms. It was something about tomorrow's breakfast, but I was too livid to care at that point. It was dark, and she was so filthy." I gritted my teeth.

"Wild mushrooms? Yeesh, sounds like Greta's the one trying to kill your guests."

Angie shot Harper a stern look then laid a calming hand on my arm and my jaw relaxed. "She's all right, though," Angie said, guiding me along, "so let's enjoy ourselves and find out about the church instead."

Pastor Basil Meyers, bundled head-to-toe for the cold night, greeted people warmly at the church doors. Except for the tie-dyed scarf around his neck, Pastor Basil seemed like an ordinary minister, middle-aged and balding under his winter cap.

"Poppy, Angie," he said bobbing his head with half-lidded eyes behind his round glasses. "Groovy, groovy. Welcome all."

Harper passed the threshold with Dewey tucked under an arm.

Pastor Basil clasped his gloved hands together. "And the mayor with Harper Tillman—far out, man. I wish I had a crowd like this on Sundays."

"Not likely," Harper muttered. She leaned in close to Angie and me. "I'm only here because of him, you know." She readjusted Mayor Dewey in her arms, clearly struggling with his girth. He gave an annoyed mew before Harper settled him in, perched half in her arms and half on one bony hip like a toddler.

"He can feel your displeasure," I said with a wry grin. "Soon, your furry mayor baby will outgrow your arms and revolt."

"He's fine," Harper quipped. "He just needs a nap."

Angie nodded toward the far side of the church. "Looks like the Founders are all together."

A crowd of townspeople from the Founders Club crowded around Jim Thornen, who appeared smug as ever, nodding and smiling and greeted each with the handshake of a slimy politician. Snippets of his smarmy voice carried to where we were standing. "As Vista Liaison, I have a dual interest…" faded into "…once a patriot, always a patriot," before disappearing into the rest of the crowd noise altogether.

"Surrounding Jim like a herd of lemmings," Harper said with a sneer. "Waiting eagerly for Jim's ego to lead them off the cliffs of sanity."

Shelby waddled up beside our small group, stuck her hands on her hips, and glared at the Founders. "Bunch of nincompoops, dearies. Falling all over themselves to be a part of that club."

"Oh, Shelby," Angie said, "I've been trying to get a hold of you about—"

Shelby continued as if she hadn't heard. "Ursula and I have an idea."

"What idea?" Harper asked quickly. "Does it involve pestering Jim?"

"The way we see it, dearies, we need our own organization." She wiggled her head with satisfaction and her beehive followed suit. "The Outlander Society."

"The Outlander Society?" I repeated, one eyebrow raised.

"That's right, dearie. Every resident who isn't a founder is welcome."

"What about me?" Angie asked. "I'm a founder, but I'm not part of Jim's club."

"Of course you're welcome, dearie. It's what's in your heart that counts."

I crossed my arms, skeptical of Shelby's intentions. "As long as what's in your heart is to harass Jim Thornen, you mean?"

"Don't discount it so quickly, dearie. And there's nothing wrong with celebrating our far-flung heritage, especially if those founders are going to throw it in our faces."

"Shelby, if I could just—" but Angie stopped short. Shelby had turned away and was already enveloped by the lingering crowd. Angie wrung her hands. "She's still avoiding me. It's those darn cinnamon rolls."

Angie's fretting reminded me of my discussion with Ryan at the diner. "I talked to Ryan earlier today."

"You did?" Angie's voice went up an octave.

"I described Randall's death to him."

"Not exactly romantic," Harper said, "but I guess it's a start."

I waved her off. "I told him about how Randall looked coming down the stairs, and Ryan thinks it may have been caused by some type of drug reaction or overdose."

Harper snorted. "It's always the stodgy old coots with the drug problems."

Angie whispered, "A drug overdose would explain why it was just him and not the others who ate my rolls. Have you told Deputy Todd?"

"Not yet."

"Well, get on it," Angie urged. "My business is taking a serious hit in the local market. I'd take you to him myself, but I can't see over the crowd." She raised on tip toes, but quickly gave up when the only one she met at eye level was Dewey.

I scanned the tops of heads for Deputy Todd's bobblehead and finally noticed it bobbing towards a back-row pew. "I'll catch up with you both later."

As I zig-zagged through the milling townspeople, I spotted Ryan seated at a pew in deep discussion with a person hidden from my view. He had a gentleness about him, that effortless laugh and knowing smile, that caught me mid-stride. I let out a deep sigh, wishing we'd had more time to talk this afternoon. How I missed our chats. It used to be me sitting next to him listening to the dulcet tones of his sweet Scottish brogue as we discussed nothing in particular. I was lost in memory as the crowd parted, revealing Ryan's seatmate. I stopped cold. Charlie Barba.

"Poppy!" a voice called through the crowd. I turned to look. Angie pointed to the back pew. "Deputy Todd," she mouthed and pointed again. "Over there."

I gave Ryan and Charlie one last doleful glance, then approached Deputy Todd.

"Good evening, Miss Lewis," he greeted me with a sour tone.

"You look like you're about as happy to be here as Harper does."

"Less, I'm sure."

I followed his gaze across the church to Jim's lemmings. Lovie tittered along with the rest and fawned at whatever words spewed from Jim's mouth. I quickly understood Deputy Todd's irritation, but I had more important matters to discuss.

"Is there any update on the toxicology report?"

"Since this morning?" he drawled. "No, why?"

I thought it best to tell him everything Ryan had shared. The details were nothing new to Deputy Todd—I'd told him everything in my interview the night of Randall's death, but Ryan's take was new. Finishing my spiel, I waited for him to respond.

"So?" was all he asked.

"So?" I repeated, confused. "So, it's not Angie's cinnamon rolls. It's not her, or her bakery that's at fault here."

He lolled his head to one side and glared up at me. "Once again, Miss Lewis, you poke your nose where it doesn't belong. I'll wait for the results of the *official* toxicology report before making any determination."

"But Angie—"

"In the meantime," he said, holding up a hand to stop me, "I suggest you find a seat. Looks like the show is about to start."

I squeeze into the pew next to Angie and Harper just as William approached the pulpit.

Angie leaned in and asked under her breath, "What did Deputy Todd say?"

"I'll fill you in later."

William cleared his throat and his eyes flickered toward the rest of the genealogy group who filled one of the front pews. Julian gave him a thumbs up and the others gave him their full attention in a show of solidarity as much as interest in the subject matter.

William straightened his leather vest and cleared his throat again, clearly nervous at being the lone center of attention for once. "A town," he began in his gruff voice, "does not come into being without its people. And a people do not make a town without a sense of community." He scanned the faces in the crowd. A cough near the back broke the dramatic silence. "The foundation we stand on," he spared a glance at the crowd again, "or sit on, I guess, pre-dates the founding of Starry Cove by almost a hundred years. And it may have all been lost to time if it weren't for the generous assistance of Starry Cove's most influential founder, a man named Claude Goodwin."

Angie let out a faint squeak, and Harper made an indistinct gurgling noise in her throat, enough to startle Dewey to the point of launching out of her arms and onto the floor.

"Keep it together," I whispered. "We'll talk afterward." But my hackles were also up at the mere mention of Claude Goodwin. Now William was going to elaborate on his existence with the whole town. Spill it all out, open the floodgates. Afterward couldn't come soon enough.

* * *

The damage, thankfully, was less than expected. After the first mention of Claude's name, William descended into a lengthy speech on old churches and their value to ancestral and genealogical pursuits.

"What are we going to do?" Angie asked as everyone got to their feet.

"Sounds like—" Harper stopped herself and waited until those around us disbursed. "Sounds like our friend Mr. Goodwin spent all his grandfather's money on projects like this."

"Maybe," I mused, watching as William joined the other genealogists and received handshakes all around.

"Should we ask him what he knows?"

"No way," Harper said. "The fewer people onto our search, the better."

"Angie may be right," I said. "We found nothing at the community center. Greta's been searching full-tilt in Arthur's library, and now at the county library, and still we haven't found anything that would tell us where Claude Goodwin may have hid his grandfather's gold. Or that there even *is* any gold. Let's not forget that."

"There better be something," Harper said, gnashing her teeth.

"And what about the Dr. Goodwin Cho mentioned?" I asked. "We know nothing about who that might be. The Gold Hand was just a few steps behind us in the forest, don't forget."

"How could we?" Angie wondered, eyes wide.

The three of us stood in silence, no doubt all remembering that day deep underground where Harper and I discovered the crypt—and skeleton—of Gold-Tooth Goodwin, Claude's grandfather. We barely scraped out alive after the Gold Hand arrived on scene.

I shook myself out of the memory. "Maybe it's time to get help from the experts."

"Fine," Harper said reluctantly, "but don't give away the farm. And we only ask William—he just mentioned Claude, so it won't seem so out of left field."

Pastor Basil and William now chatted by the far wall. With a game plan in place, we mustered our courage and approached in our best casual gaits. We were just a few residents with typical resident questions for the presenter.

William greeted us as we maneuvered beside him and the pastor. "I hope you all enjoyed this little history lesson."

"It was enlightening," I said, briefly glancing at Harper and Angie at my side, "to say the least."

"It was far out, man," Pastor Basil said, bobbing his head. "A total gas, man. Blew my mind."

"It's so, uh, interesting to hear these old stories." I hoped my voice sounded nonchalant. "And it's so, um, fortunate that nice man stepped in to fund restoration of the church."

Harper and Angie both nodded vigorously, eyeing William.

"By the grace of God," Pastor Basil said. "And by the bread in the deep pockets of the faithful," he added with a wink.

"Yes," William agreed. "The wealthy often stepped in to preserve public buildings, but it wasn't always out of good will. If the church was disused, they'd either have to pay for a new one or the people would up and leave, and that would mean no more workers for their industries. Better to chip in for repairs."

"You seemed to sing this man... What was his name?"

"Claude Goodwin," William said.

"Yes, him," I continued. "You seemed to sing his praises earlier."

"That I did, because the fact is, without him, I doubt this town would still exist."

"Do you know anything else about him?" Angie asked in her tiniest voice.

"Just that he was a wealthy man and founder here in this town. Once I get my hands on the church bibles and those town records, I may be able to tell you more."

That seemed to add a spark of energy to Pastor Basil. "No sweat, man. The records are ready. Some buttoned-up square came by a few weeks ago asking to look at them, so the older ones are already pulled out of storage."

William seemed stunned. "Who was he?"

Pastor Basil twisted his lips. "Can't say I remember. He was decked out in a suit and had an English name, you dig?"

"Randall Portsmouth." The name dripped like sludge from beneath William's bushy mustache.

Pastor Basil snapped his fingers. "That's the one."

My stomach sank. "Randall was my guest who died."

"Oh," Pastor Basil said, his enthusiasm gone, "I had no idea."

"Typical Randall," William spat, "jumping ahead of everyone to get the best bits for his own manuscript."

"I'd appreciate anything you could learn about this Claude Goodwin."

"Randall probably ripped out all the good pages."

Pastor Basil took a step back. "Ripped them out?"

William grunted. "I wouldn't put it past him. Anything to deny others the opportunity, selfish bas—"

"There you are, Poppy!" a woman called out. Candace was upon us in an instant. "We're heading back to the bed-and-breakfast. I've got a hankering for some tea and cookies but this place only has water and wafer crackers, and the wine's probably all locked up." She winked then cackled at her own joke. "Anyway, I was hoping to get ahold of those town files tomorrow, since you were kind enough to haul them out already."

My eyes met Harper's for an instant before I replied. "I'm not sure if they're available yet. You'll have to ask Harper Tillman." I nodded to Harper, and she scowled before Candace turned her way.

"Well then?" Candace asked Harper.

"I'd like a crack at them, too," William said. "I'm sure we all would."

Harper froze for only a moment, then said, "I'll, uh, have to check with the mayor."

Williams's face bore a look of confusion. "Isn't your mayor a cat?"

Harper shrugged. "Protocols."

"Hmm," Candace muttered, eyes narrowing. "All right then. I saw the little guy around here somewhere. Ah, there. Yeardley has him."

Yeardley approached the group with Mayor Dewey writhing in her arms. He pushed against her attempts at hugs and snuggles. "He's a feisty one," she said.

Harper nearly choked and snatched him from Yeardley's grasp. He immediately settled and tucked his nose into the crook of her bony elbow. "He's probably just tired."

Yeardley brushed the fur off her sweater. "Reminds me of my Mr. Mittens—nothing but pointy ends." A sadness came over her face and Candace gave her a gentle squeeze.

William nodded to the cat nestled in Harper's arms. "Now that the mayor's here, can we ask for access to those records?"

Harper shot me a quick glance, and I inclined my head in surrender.

"How does tomorrow sound?" Harper asked.

Candace clapped once. "Perfect. We'll be in town a few more days, it seems. That deputy of yours practically snapped my head off when I asked about his investigation."

Angie tugged at my sleeve and nudged me away. We excused ourselves in a rush, leaving Candace, William, and Pastor Basil to the rest of their conversation.

Once we were at a safe distance, Harper scoffed at me. "I can't believe you threw me under the bus like that."

"Never mind that," Angie cut in. "What did Deputy Todd say? I was so wrapped up in Claude Goodwin I forgot to ask."

I put on my best positive face. "He said they're still investigating."

She looked crestfallen. "But what about what Ryan said?"

I chose my words carefully. "He didn't discount it. He just said that he has to wait for the official toxicology results." I twisted my face into what I hoped looked like a supportive smile. That was all technically true.

"So, we're back where we were," Harper said, "and Angie's still on the roster."

I shook my head. Something didn't line up. "But now we know Randall came to town a few weeks ago. Why would he do that if he knew he'd be here for the event?"

"Maybe William is right and Randall was a royal jerk."

"I don't doubt that," I said. "But William looked ready to spit nails when Pastor Basil told him Randall had already gone through the church records. Julian wasn't wrong about them—those two hated each other." I scanned the assembly and spotted William schmoozing a cluster of women. Hate could go a long, long way.

Eleven

"YOU DIDN'T HAVE to scare them," I said to Greta as we washed up after breakfast the next day. "You could have just said they were a type of mushrooms."

"What's the fun in that?"

"It's not meant to be fun."

"Bah! Suit yourself, but the look on that bearded fella's face was worth it."

Wanting to keep my voice firm, I stifled a snicker as I remembered William's bugged eyes when Greta told him the dish was Hedgehog Frittata. I changed the subject instead. "Are you going to the library today?"

Greta hopped off her stool in front of the sink and wiped her hands dry on her drab dress. "If you'll release my chains."

I prayed for patience. "For that last time, you are not a prisoner here. You can go now. I'll take care of the rooms."

My cell phone rang as Greta rushed from the kitchen. I dried my hands on a clean tea towel before pulling it from the back pocket of my jeans. "Hello?"

"It's Harper. I finally got around to checking Mayor Dewey's mail and you'll never guess what I found."

"What do you mean by 'finally'?" I asked with not a small amount of displeasure.

"Anyway," Harper continued, brushing aside my admonishment, "I found a letter from Randall Portsmouth asking to review the town records."

"So, he tried after all."

"Yep. Like, two weeks ago."

"You haven't checked Mayor Dewey's mail for two weeks?"

"Three, actually, but I'm getting to it now. I even found that stupid letter from the county about Jim."

"You *deliver* his mail, Harper."

"I've been busy, okay? Dewey's had a lot of social obligation. And SCAT is tomorrow—ugh."

"Is the community center ready?" I asked. "We've finished up breakfast and I think my guests are all about to head your way."

"Yeah, I'm in the Town Hall office now. I just unlocked the place. Your flock of history buffs can fly right in."

"Great. I'm going to clean up here then I might head over to chaperone. Talk to you later."

As I hung up the phone and exited the kitchen, a train of my guests was already headed out the front door.

"Off we go," Candace said, waving cheerfully.

Shutting the door behind them, I headed upstairs to service the rooms, but noise from Julian's suite stopped me at the top stair. I'd heard Greta zooming off on the scooter, so I knew it couldn't be her. I crept along the landing to the door and peeked through the opening.

Olivia's long braid swung as she riffled through the box of Randall's belongings. She pulled out papers and tossed them wildly onto the sprawling bed, digging deeper into the box. I remembered my confrontation with Everett, but unlike him, Olivia had no reason to be in there.

I burst into the room. "What's going on here?" I demanded.

Olivia turned as stared at me with a level look. "Nothing that concerns you."

I equaled her gaze. "Everyone's gone and you are rummaging through my guest's room. That concerns me. And with Randall pointing a finger at you as he died, it looks pretty bad from my end."

Olivia straightened. "I'm just taking back what's mine."

"This belongs to Randall."

Olivia let out a mocking laugh. "None of this," she gripped a sheaf of papers in her fist, "belongs to Randall."

"What's that supposed to mean?"

"It's complicated," she said with a sneer. "But this is mine."

"Did you do something to Randall?" The allegation was out of my mouth before I could stop it, but what she was doing here was more than suspicious. "Why did he accuse you with his dying breath?"

Olivia took a step back and her mouth sank into a frown before resolve overcame her face once more. "I don't know what that was about, I swear, but Randall deserved whatever happened to him—choking on a cinnamon roll, heart attack, falling down the stairs." Olivia sneered. "Couldn't have happened to a nicer guy."

This woman, whom I first thought reminded me of myself, was horrible. Callous, even. How had I been so wrong in our first impression? "How can you say that?"

"Everyone's thinking the same thing, whether or not they say it aloud. Maybe Ivy or Julian wouldn't have it in them to wish Randall dead, but the rest of us could."

I stepped closer. "What happened?"

She met my stare, eye for eye. "Like most privileged men, Randall is—was—a bully." She leaned her head gently to the side then addressed someone behind me. "Right, Ivy?" she asked in a raised voice.

I turned and spotted Ivy on the landing outside the door and she ventured over, easing the door aside to enter.

"What's that?" she asked, going wide-eyed at the mess of papers on the bed.

"That Randall was a bully." Olivia was addressing me now. "He was trying to maneuver himself to take over our little society."

"Candace already told me," I said. "You were there, Ivy. Was Randall really that bad?"

Ivy stared down at her broken arm, which she cradled with the other. "He—" she stuttered. "He was quite aggressive."

Olivia scoffed. "Thought he'd make a better leader than Julian. He was pushing hard, not that anyone would vote for him." She stopped suddenly and regarded Ivy more closely. "Are you all right? You look terrible."

Ivy made little reaction, but addressed me meekly, "Excuse me, Miss Lewis, I came back because I was hoping you might have some aspirin." She regarded her cradled arm. "It's not usually this bad. Maybe I just need to lie down."

"Of course," I said. "I'm sure I have some extra-strength pills around here somewhere." My eyes swiveled to Olivia, and I raised an eyebrow to indicate her soiree in the Victorian room was over.

***

Ursula phoned mid-morning to let me know my order had finally come in at the general store, so I donned my puffy coat and hit the sidewalk. My strides took me past the hardware store where I spotted Trevor deep in conversation at the front counter. I happened a quick glance as I passed the glass door into the shop and stopped cold. A colorful flyer, neatly taped to the glass at top and bottom, advertised the upcoming Founders Club. Upon closer look, I gritted my teeth. "Founders only! No non-founders allowed," it read.

I ripped the flyer off the door and pushed through to the store. Trevor stopped mid-sentence and stared at me in surprise as I waved the flyer in front of his face. "What is this?" I demanded.

Trevor looked shocked. "It's for the meeting tonight."

"No," I said, "what is *this*?" I pointed to the part disallowing non-founders.

Trevor leaned in close and squinted, then said calmly, "Well, it just means the meeting ain't for them." He straightened and addressed the man he'd been speaking to when I barged in. "Ain't that right?"

I gave a start when I realize it was William standing next to us. He wore a thick leather jacket and his beard flowed down the front. I wondered if he ever got it stuck in the zipper.

William patted his stomach and puffed out his mustache. "That's correct. I've been asked to facilitate a short discussion on the early families in the region."

"And," Trevor said proudly, looping his thumbs over the straps of his overalls, "I'm going to learn about the tonsorial arts. Did you know barbers were usually town leaders, too? On account of all the training and such."

I peered around at the goods on offer at the hardware store. "You can't give haircuts with garden clippers, Trevor."

Trevor opened his mouth to respond, but the door opened behind us and Marty Hardy, the mechanic, walked in. "Whose hog is that out front? Have you upgraded from your scooter, Poppy?"

"That'd be mine," William said.

Marty seemed impressed. "You been riding a long time?"

"Nearly thirty years, I'd say." William leaned back on his boot heels and stretched his arms out. The leather of his jacket creaked.

"Is that a Harley-Davidson Super Glide?"

William's eyes widen for a moment and a heel gave way. He quickly regained his footing and mumbled something to the effect of, "Mm-hmm."

Marty let out a low whistle. "Impressive. What wheels did you go with?"

"Uh, just the, you know, basic kind."

Marty tilted his head to the side. "Thought I saw custom bars, too."

"Custom, uh…" William quickly turned his focus back to Trevor, who beamed back at him, impressed.

"Been riding with the Lone Wolves out of Vista. Tough group, those guys."

Trevor nodded, knowingly, but I frowned, doubting he had any clue what William was talking about. Marty crossed his arms and regarded William with silent consideration.

"Anyway," William said, rushing toward the door, "lots of records to go through. Just stopped by for a quick chat."

As the door clanged behind William, Marty turned back to us. "I didn't want to say anything, but that man didn't make a lick of sense."

"Sounded real impressive to me," Trevor said, tapping at the flyer where I'd slapped it down on the counter. "Can't wait for tonight."

"What's tonight?" Marty asked.

I scooped up the flyer and shoved it into his hands. "An exclusive club meeting. You and I aren't invited."

Marty read the flyer, then frowned, turning a disapproving look toward Trevor. "Sounds kind of mean-spirited, leaving others out."

"Jim's idea," I said.

"That's not what it's about at all," Trevor said.

"Sounds like that's exactly what it's about."

"Now, Marty, don't get upset. Jim just wants to celebrate those of us who have real history in this town."

Marty's disapproving look turned to anger. "Real history, huh? Is my workshop imaginary to you?"

My hand shot up, stopping Trevor from responding, and I stepped between the two men. "That's enough. You two are friends, remember?" Neither man said a word. "Remember?" I repeated with more force.

Marty finally turned his stare away from Trevor. "You're right, Poppy," he said, "but I suddenly realize I don't want anything from the hardware store."

Trevor grunted. "Fine by me."

I followed Marty out the door, stopping him on the sidewalk. "Do you know anything about the Lone Wolves motorcycle gang?"

Marty shook his head. "Sorry, Poppy. I'm the wrong person to ask about that sort of thing." We said our good-byes, and he turned away toward his workshop.

I still needed to pick up my order from Ursula, so I popped next door to the general store. Maybe Ryan would be free for lunch.

I spotted him behind the pharmacy glass in the back, but as I approached, I realized he was on the phone. I only caught the end of the conversation.

"No, no, I understand," Ryan said, squeezing his eyes shut and rubbing his temple. "Aye, Mrs. Grubber, I know this is the third time this month. I'll be there right away." He hung up the phone and seemed to perk up when he spotted me waiting nearby.

"Hi there," I said. "Thought I'd pop by and see if you wanted to grab lunch, but sounds like you've got other plans. Your son again?"

He was already peeling off his white lab coat. To-day's V-neck sweater was navy blue. "Aye, sorry, Poppy. He's been an absolute roaster lately." He replaced the lab coat with a thicker jacket and avoided eye contact while putting it on. "You aren't thinking of having lunch with, uh, that Cesar fellow, are you?"

I raised an eyebrow. "I hadn't planned on it. Why?"

"Er," Ryan muttered, "no reason. Just making

conversation." He finally looked up but didn't catch my eye. "Looks like Ursula's got something for you."

I followed his gaze to Ursula's counter. She'd stacked a few boxes and waited patiently. "Must be my order."

"Well," he said, not moving, "I guess I should be going."

"Oh, right," I mumbled, stepping aside. He was almost to the door when I called back. "This town could be good for him. Your son, I mean."

Ryan smiled back. "Aye, I know."

Ursula stared at the door after Ryan disappeared. "Poor man," she said. "That son of his is causing quite a ruckus."

"Probably just going through a phase," I responded. I didn't actually have any clue, since I had no children of my own, but it sounded like something an adult would say about an adolescent.

"Kids need to keep busy—and not with video games, mind you. They need to get outside. Sports, hobbies, that sort of thing."

"Do you know Ethan well?"

"He's come in a few times."

"I haven't even been introduced."

"Well now," Ursula said, "I wouldn't read too much into that."

I managed to grunt a response, not sure if I believed her. What was wrong with me? I wasn't scary. I didn't bite.

"When my son was younger, he was a troublemaker, too."

"Not your son? He was so polite when he came to

visit last month."

Ursula nodded sagely. "Caused me a lot of grief. Finally found him a hobby that he latched on to. Kept him busy, and he finally grew out of the trouble, but it was touch and go for a while."

"What hobby?" I asked, curious.

Ursula smiled with a twinkle in her eye. "Woodworking. My brother, Stan, put a drill in his hand one day and that was all it took. Couldn't get him out of the work shed. He must have built me ten birdhouses that first summer." She shook her head and chuckled at the memory.

"Woodworking," I repeated, eyes narrowing. "Interesting."

Twelve

WITH NO LUNCH plans, I decided to hit the road and dig a little deeper into William's sketchy story. I knew next to nothing about motorcycle gangs, but as luck would have it, I knew a guy—a couple of guys, actually. And I bet my pink overalls there was a pretty good sandwich waiting for me, too.

The Vista Tavern was a crumbled old stand-alone building on the wrong side of the proverbial Vista tracks. No windows, a cracked sign, and a wide berth of any upstanding citizens. I rolled my hybrid Prius to a stop next to a line of beefy motorcycles parked in the gravel lot in front.

It was drizzly at mid-day, so the transition from the daylight outside to the near total darkness inside was less of a shock. I let the door close behind me and let my eyes adjust. A layer of smoke lingered in the air.

"Poppy!" came a roar from the bar.

"Hey, Joe," I said, blinking a few times before grabbing a stool at the counter. "I'll have a beer and one of those hot chicken sandwiches."

Joe slapped the bar and grinned. "As the lady says."

"Well look at what we got here," another voice called from nearby. "If it ain't the innkeeper herself."

"Hey Gus. Hank." I nodded to the two men seated at the other end of the bar, nearer to the television mounted in the corner. "How've you been?"

"Surviving," Hank said from underneath his greasy ball cap. "You opened that bed-and-breakfast yet?"

I couldn't hold back a smile. "I have my first set of guests right now."

"In that case," Joe announced, "beer's on the house."

"Thanks, Joe. I'm also here because I was hoping you guys might be able to help."

Hank and Gus both turned in their stools to face me directly. Gus raised a bushy eyebrow. "You got another mystery on your hands?"

"Sort of. Have either of you heard of the Lone Wolves motorcycle gang? I have a guest who swears he's part of this gang out of Vista, but I'm not so sure."

Their faces were blank, and for a moment I thought they hadn't understood what I was asking. Then Hank slapped Gus on the back and they both erupted in laughter. Joe chuckled as he dried a pint glass with a towel.

"First off," Hank said, wiping a tear away from his eye, "if he's callin' it a gang, then it ain't no gang."

I looked to Joe in confusion, and he said, "The term is club. Anyone who says they're in a motorcycle gang doesn't know the first thing about 'em."

That made sense. "So you think he's lying?"

"Mm-hmm," Gus mumbled. "Either that or he's just plain stupid. What kind of motorcycle's this guy got?"

I tried to recall what Marty had called it. "A Super Slide?"

"Super Glide," Hank sneered. "Typical. Probably some blow hard goin' through a mid-life crisis. What's this fella up to?"

"It's not that he's up to something," I said, "but lying about this is suspicious."

Gus piped up, "Who names their fake motorcycle club the Lone Wolves, anyway?"

Joe slapped down another pint in front of Gus. "Someone who rides alone." The three of them burst into howls of laughter once again, settling down after a moment with a few rough coughs washed down with swigs of beer.

I ate my sandwich between bouts of banter with the guys and shared stories of the Pearl's renovation process. The bed-and-breakfast had been in the throes of renovation the last time I'd stopped into the Vista Tavern, and it was nice to catch up with the guys. But between the conversation, my mind fell back to wondering about William. If he could lie about this, what else might he be lying about? It appeared to be common knowledge that he and Randall hated one another, but I wasn't convinced William was bold enough to take action—possibly murder—with all eyes watching.

Gus interrupted my thoughts. "You ought to come by more often, Poppy. Hank and I get lonely watching this sad excuse for a television with just Joe for company."

"Your drinks keep you company," Joe shot back.

"Yeah," Hank said to me, "and if you got any more guests with make believe motorcycle gangs, you let us know." That brought chuckles all around.

"You'll be the first ones to know," I said, slapping a tip on the counter for Joe. "But I've got to head out. Lots to do."

"Take care, Poppy. I don't like that you got these lyin' bums staying at your place."

"Thanks Joe, but I'll be okay."

He tilted his head in acknowledgement. "All right, but you know who to call if you need anything."

Hank and Gus nodded in agreement, and I felt reassured that I had them on my side should anything turn south. But the scariest thing I had on my plate right then was Greta's unsupervised excursions out in public. And I figured that while I was in Vista, I might just pay her a surprise visit.

***

I pulled into the Vista County Library parking lot and immediately clenched my teeth. The scooter was parked near the front entrance, sideways, across the dividing line of two parking spaces. Rolling into the open space next to it, I climbed out of the car and trudged inside.

A kindly looking woman with brown hair tied in a wispy bun sat in a high stool behind the checkout counter. Her eyes swiveled up from the hefty book she'd been reading when I approached. The last time I was here, the librarian had been incredibly helpful, guiding me through their digital records. That's how I learned about the old town of Prosper Hollow, the precursor to the logging town of Prosperity, the ruins in which Harper and I had discovered the hidden tomb of Gold-Tooth Goodwin. Now, I was hopeful I'd find a similar level of assistance.

"Hi there," I said in my quietest library voice. "I'm

wondering if you've seen an old lady in here. Gray dress, wild hair."

"Oh," she said with a displeased flatness her voice. "Does she belong to you?"

I cringed. "Sorry."

The librarian dropped the book on the counter with a thump and pursed her lips. "This isn't an adult daycare, you know. There are services for that." With the same exasperated look on her face, she reached below the counter then handed me a pamphlet.

"Thanks," I said, taking the brochure. Glancing at it, I winced again. *Adult Day Services for Busy Lives.* "Where can I find her?"

The librarian shot a thumb toward a row of books in the far corner. A plain white sign stuck on the side of a nearby bookcase identified it as the non-fiction section. "She was in 265 earlier, but now I think she's migrated to 978."

"Pardon?"

She heaved a sigh as if she'd explained this a thousand times before. "Dewey Decimals. She's in the 900 section somewhere."

"Got it," I said, and hurried away. Checking down each row, it was a light humming that finally guided me to Greta's hiding spot. I turned the corner of the history section and stopped. Far down the line, stacks of books towered at varying heights on the floor in a semi-circle, effectively cordoning off the end of the row as it ended against the wall. Greta sat on the floor behind the barrier. Gray hair stuck out between the straps of the scooter helmet she still wore.

I scurried along the row between the bookcases until

I was nearly on top of her. "What are you doing?" I demanded in a harsh whisper, looking over my shoulder to make sure there were no other patrons nearby. "You cannot build forts in the library."

Greta did not look up. Instead, she held up a single gnarled index finger to silence me, then finished muttering a line of text from the oversized book that lay in her lap. Plucking one long strand of her hair, she laid it gently along the spine to mark her place, then shut the book. "Yes?" she asked, gazing up at me as if nothing were the matter.

"Why…" I couldn't formulate words through my frustration. "Why are you still wearing your helmet?"

Greta looked taken aback at this question. "Because you told me I had to wear it at all times."

"Not when you're inside. I meant when you're riding the scooter."

"Well then," she said, snapping off the chin strap. "Suit yourself."

"And why is the scooter taking up two parking spots? I thought we talked about this."

"I parked on the line so it wouldn't take up *any* spots. Pretty sure I left enough room for cars to squeeze in on either side."

A small growl escaped my throat.

"I thought you'd appreciate my prudence."

I closed my eyes and waited for my anger to subside, working on the deep breathing techniques Angie taught me, then picked up the top book off the tallest pile. "Composition of the Human Body," I said, reading off the title. "What is this? What have you found?"

She waved a hand at the piles of books. "Load of

nonsense, most of it." She twisted around and hefted a book from a smaller pile off to the side. "Did you know a body takes eight to twelve years to fully decompose? Much faster if disposed of by sea. We should remember that."

A scoff of disgust came from behind me. I turned around to see a bespectacled woman staring at us with a look of revulsion on her face. She quickly stuffed a book into its place on the shelf, frowned and rushed away.

"Ugh. Have you found anything useful?"

She motioned toward the book I held. "The human body contains trace elements of gold. But nothing specifically about 'golden blood' or hidden treasure, if that's what you're asking."

Greta's head darted to the side like a bird, staring daggers at something behind me. A young girl meandered partway down the row and perused the books on the shelf. Her finger followed a line of titles, clearly looking for a specific volume.

"Occupied!" Greta snapped. The girl jumped, startled at the shout, and ran from the row.

"Maybe this was a bad idea." I felt the frown lines between my eyes growing deeper. "I'm not sure it's worth the trouble having you come all the way out here to play fort and snap at kids."

Greta sucked in her breath and wiggled as if I'd ruffled her feathers.

"And maybe my guests will find something in the records you've already reviewed at the community center."

This really must have pinched a nerve, because Greta's face waned between incredulity and renewed conviction. She responded sternly in a loud voice. "I don't care if a hundred gynecologists ferret around in our private business. They won't find anything exciting, that's for sure. And I've got a mind to dig as far as I can until I find the treasure, even if it is hidden in some old musty cave."

"Ahem." Behind me and down at the entrance to the row was the messy-bunned librarian. Her eyes were flat and emotionless as if drained of energy as they scanned the many teetering towers of books Greta had pulled from the shelves. She let out a single heavy sigh. "I don't suppose you plan on checking out any of those books."

"Um," I said, glancing toward the fort with a frown. "possibly."

The librarian leaned her head to one side and lolled her dead eyes to look at me. "Really?" she drawled.

Probably not, I admitted to myself, but my trip to the library didn't have to be a total bust. "Actually," I said after a moment, "could you help me find a book?"

The woman face turned to stunned surprise. "Really?" she repeated, lively this time.

"Yeah," I said with a smile, a plan already taking shape in my head.

***

After telling Greta for what I hoped was the final time that the guests were genealogists, not gynecologists, I installed her in the library back at the house. Most of the guests were still at the community center or relaxing in the mansion's common room. Only Everett was in the library when we arrived and Greta plopped reluctantly in the remaining club chair, staring daggers at him. He did not seem to notice, and continued to flip through a nondescript volume of some mundane subject, I was sure.

I retreated to my room to will the oncoming migraine to pass me by. I laid down on the bed and closed my eyes and a gentle calmness washed over me. But before long thoughts crept back in. The Victorian chair, its upholstery ripped from the back, sat in the corner—I could imagine it through my eyelids. After staring at it over time, the map scrawled into the wood of the back panel was seared into my memory.

So much for my nap. Instead, I sat on the floor by the chair and inspected the map as I'd done so many times before. I traced the trail of lines with my finger and bit on my bottom lip. It sure looked like a treasure map. A sinuous line reached across the panel, starting at one end and winding its way to the other. An actual X marked an end point of the line and other symbols tracked its path. The question was, what did they mean and where was the starting point? "Where are you?" I wondered aloud, tapping the X. "Where is your treasure, Claude?"

The truth was, we only assumed it was a treasure map. With all the stories of gold surrounding Claude Goodwin's pirate grandfather, and Claude's enormous wealth, we hoped this collection of dotted lines and cryptic notes led to a pile of riches. But for all we were certain, it could lead to Claude Goodwin's favorite fishing hole and the only treasure we'd find were goldfish.

I leaned back, resting against my bed with my feet crossed on the floor. It wasn't a lot to go on, just a squiggly line and some cryptic hieroglyphics. I thought about asking the historians before quickly dismissing the idea with a shake of my head. The last thing we needed was the scrutiny and circus that could follow if word got out that there was hidden treasure in Starry Cove.

Thirteen

ANGIE SLAPPED THE newspaper on the counter in a puff of finely ground white flour. "It's shameful," she said, blotches of red overtaking her neck and cheeks. "This is all Jim's doing. He's tearing this town apart."

Harper finished her scone by shoving the rest in her mouth. "Not surprising," she mumbled through the crumbs. "Jim's ego will bulldoze anything that impinges on his power."

"Let me see this article." I snatched the paper off the counter and scanned for Veronica Valentine's article. I found it near the bottom of the front page, Veronica's skeevy smirk soiling the accompanying picture.

Founders Versus Outlanders: Starry Cove's Grudge Match Continues

In what seemed the highlight of the month's social calendar, Starry Cove kicked off its inaugural Founders Club meeting last night to a packed crowd. Packed, that is, with town founders only. None of the so-called 'outlanders' were allowed into the town's exclusive club, reserved for residents whose ancestry can be traced back to the official founding of Starry Cove in 1879.

No word on how the outlanders spent their evening, but the Founders took the opportunity to draft a charter and distribute badges to all founding family members. Visiting genealogist and historian, William Boyd, offered a glimpse into the old west when he presented slides depicting the town's roots in the fishing and logging industries.

Former Mayor, Jim Thornen, spearheaded the effort to recognize the contributions of the founding families and to bring together "a kinship that will last into the next century of Starry Cove and beyond."

"Kinship," I squawked. "Jim wouldn't know kinship if it gave him a big sloppy kiss."

"Harper, isn't there anything you can do?"

Harper nearly choked on her coffee. "Me?" she asked. "What am I supposed to do?"

"Oh, I don't know," Angie said. "Get Dewey to stop it."

"What's he going to do? Nap the controversy away? Pat it away like a toy mouse?"

"It's just so frustrating." Angie stomped one tiny foot. "You know, I heard Jim catered the event with some bakery in Vista. Can you believe that?"

I shrugged. "I guess supporting your town only goes so far."

"Yeah," Harper said, "about as far as who your great-great-grandfather was. And wasn't Jim's relative basically the town jester?"

"General laborer," I corrected.

"Who owed Claude Goodwin quite a bit of money," Harper added.

"That's right," Angie fumed. "A far cry from the upstanding citizen he plays now."

Harper leaned back in her chair with a sneer on her face. "We'll see if he shows his face at SCAT tonight."

Movement at the front window caught Angie's eye. "Oh, oh, a customer." She scurried behind the counter. "It's been dead since your guest… died. Sorry, that wasn't what I meant to say."

"It's all right," I said, but Angie's face fell when I added, "but I think it's just Shelby."

Sure enough, a moment later, Shelby and her beehive tottered through the bakery door. She waved a rolled-up newspaper as if about to swat an unruly child. "Can you believe this bunkum? Founders my donkey, dearies."

"We saw," I said.

"Lovie's heads about as big as a three-ton pig and a few of them *Founders* waddled in wearing gaudy oversized pins like clowns at a carnival."

Angie jabbed her fists on her hips. "I'm surprised you'd show your face in here, the way you've been avoiding me lately."

"Avoiding you?" Shelby let out a nervous chuckle.

"That's right. You've barely said two words to me

since that poor man died. We're supposed to be starting a business. How do you expect that to work?"

"Well now, dearie. Don't take it personally. I wouldn't do business with anyone if their food was deadly."

Angie's mouth worked in silently from the blow.

Harper sat up and jabbed a finger at Shelby. "You know Angie had nothing to do with that."

"Who then, dearies?"

Before any of us could respond, Cesar popped his head through the door from the kitchen. "Hello there," he said. "Thought I heard a few people. Hi Poppy." He nodded toward me with a smile.

Harper let out an exasperated sigh. "Buzz off, Cesar. Poppy's busy."

Cesar ducked quickly back into the kitchen and Shelby's eyes followed him. I shot Harper a vexed look, and she shrugged.

"Angie," Shelby said, "didn't you say Roy was out of town?"

"Yes, his mother is ill."

"So, that means Cesar's been doing a lot of the baking?"

Angie's eyes widened. "I can't believe you would even think Cesar had anything to do with this."

"He hasn't been acting strange at all, has he?" Shelby asked.

Angie stammered, but then took a moment to think. "He did come back from lunch a few days ago whistling and humming to himself. I'd never heard him whistle before. He was at your diner, though. Did you see anything?"

Shelby looked toward me. "He was having lunch with Poppy. Did you notice anything?"

Cesar had been cheerful—overly so—but he wasn't maniacal or murderous. "I don't think so."

"How thick are you all?" Harper snapped. "Cesar's got the hots for Poppy, duh. He's just in a lovey-dovey daze."

Their faces all turned my way, and I wilted under their stares, then tried to change the subject. "Angie's food isn't deadly. Deputy Todd said my guest didn't die from choking."

Shelby threw up her hands. "That's news to me, dearie. Look, Angie, let's let the hubbub die down a bit before we carry on, okay? It's not a good look right now."

Angie huffed. "All right. But you have to promise me we're just waiting it out."

"I promise, dearie," Shelby said in her sweetest voice, waving as she exited the bakery.

"She's got some nerve," Harper said after the door came to a close. "I guess she forgot about the chicken cacciatore special she served last year. Nearly the whole town got food poisoning. I was out of commission for a week."

"Don't mind her, Angie."

"Thanks," she mumbled. "Hey, how did the community center search go? I saw a bunch of your guests wander by yesterday."

"I prodded each of them last night," I said, "but there weren't any bites. Nothing about Claude Goodwin, at least not yet. But I found out William's been lying to everyone."

"Lying?" Harper asked. "About what?"

"He tells everyone he's in a motorcycle gang. And

that's his motorcycle parked in front of the Pearl. But Marty and my friends in Vista seem to think he's making it all up. His gang—club—doesn't exist."

"Maybe he's just some sad middle-aged dude who needs to pretend he's cool."

"I just know that he and Randall were sworn enemies. And if he's been lying to everyone about this, what else is he lying about?"

"You think he may be responsible for Randall?" Angie asked.

I shrugged. "Who knows at this point? I caught Olivia and Everett going through Randall's things, too."

Harper tsked. "What a shady bunch. Maybe they all did it."

"I suppose that's possible, too," I said. "I stepped out that morning and left them at the house. Greta was in the library, but I'm sure she didn't bother to keep tabs on anyone. And we don't even know what *it* was yet. Deputy Todd hasn't come back with any tox results."

"How'd you find out about William?" Angie asked.

"At the hardware store. I was on my way to Ursula's and I stopped in."

"Did you see Ryan?" Angie asked casually.

"More son troubles."

Angie frowned. "Oh no, that's too bad."

"That's what boarding school is for," Harper said flippantly. "Save yourself the headache."

"So I went to Vista for lunch then stopped at the library to check on Greta."

They must have seen the scowl on my face because Angie asked, "What happened?"

"Just… Greta. You know?"

They both nodded. They knew.

"How did her foraged mushrooms go over?"

Harper quickly added, "I hope you checked to make sure they weren't poisonous."

"Fine," I said, "after the guests understood what they were eating."

"I wonder if I could forage juniper berries?"

"Probably," I said. "Are you going to make Bruno's bread?"

"I might dabble." The twinkle in her eye told me she'd already dabbled. "Besides," she said, sighing. "I need something to take my mind off my sagging sales."

"I'll talk to William," I said to reassure her. "At least it's something we can do while we wait for the final results. Don't worry yourself, Angie. Concentrate on recreating that famous family recipe."

***

The sun had emerged from the clouds, giving the winter day a much-needed ray of light and warmth. I assumed the group would still be entrenched at the house, including William.

I turned the corner to approached the kitchen door off the side of the house and saw Candace and Yeardley whispering on a bench in the sunlight. They hadn't noticed me, so I tucked behind a bit of evergreen foliage and listened. I caught the last of what Yeardley was saying.

"—that Olivia knows."

Candace placed a hand on Yeardley's knee. "Who cares?" Yeardley swatted Candace's hand, and she pulled back as if bitten.

"We should be more discreet." Yeardley twisted

away from Candace and placed a hand on a bag at her side. It slouched in a rectangular shape and I suspected that was her manuscript. But that hand on Yeardley's knee had more than a twinge of familiarity to it. They must be hiding a relationship from the others. The others might miss it, but it didn't surprise me that Olivia sussed it out. I couldn't stay hidden forever, so I straightened my coat and stepped into the open.

"Hi there," I said, approaching the two.

Both women looked startled at my appearance and adjusted themselves to create more space between them on the bench.

"Lovely morning, Poppy," Candace chimed. "Didn't think we'd see this much sun."

"It's a nice day to be outside." I looked around the property. "Don't see anyone else, though. Are the rest inside?"

"I'm sure they are," Yeardley said. "I haven't seen anyone leave."

"Oh, I thought I heard someone talking to Olivia. Or at least, I heard her name."

Candace and Yeardley exchanged knowing glances.

"Not out here," Yeardley said finally.

"Ah," I said, nodding my head slowly, "my mistake. She has been acting strangely, though, hasn't she?"

"Strange?" Candace asked. "I'm not sure what you mean."

"For starters, she didn't go with the rest of you to the community center yesterday. Isn't that strange?"

Yeardley scoffed and tightened her scarf against her neck. "Not if you know Olivia. She always does as she pleases."

"Mm," Candace murmured in agreement.

"I never escorted her upstairs. Never got a chance to settle her in her room."

Candace waved me off. "You were busy. I showed her to her room. She was the only one left, after all. Always late."

"Right." I slowly nodded, but I kept thinking back to Olivia in Randall's room. What had she been searching for? And he seemed to single her out as he lay dying. "Don't you think it odd that Randall would point right at her in his last moments?"

"Well," Candace said, lowering her voice, "I didn't want to insinuate, but Randall also mumbled something that sounded like an accusation to me."

"I heard it, too," said Yeardley. "He said it was her."

"Can either of you remember if Olivia did anything strange when she arrived? Or while I was gone for a short period that first morning?"

"Let's see," Candace said, tapping her chin and staring off into the bushes. "I showed her upstairs—I remember pointing out the architecture. Olivia always liked these old houses. She asked who she was sharing a room with, and I told her it was Ivy."

"Did you tell her where the others were sleeping?"

Candace's mouth dipped into a considering frown. "I think I said Julian and Randall were across the landing since that's where you took Julian. There was only one other room, so that had to be Everett and William."

"Nothing strange?"

Shaking her head, Candace seemed to dismiss the idea. "I left for a minute or two to grab a sweater from my own room, but when I returned, she was still settling in.

Nothing strange."

After a moment, Yeardley asked, "Do you think she's done something?"

I smiled to reassure her. "I just think it's strange, is all. No matter. I'm actually looking for William. Is he inside?"

"I'm not sure," Candace said and stood up. "We'll join you. We were just about to head inside, weren't we?"

"Yes," Yeardley said. She placed a hand on the armrest of the bench and lifted herself up before falling back into the seat. "Oof," she said, placing a hand to her temple.

Candace rushed to Yeardley's side and grabbed her arm to steady her.

"Are you all right?" I asked.

"I'm fine," she replied. "Just a little woozy."

"Let's get you a snack," Candace said, easing Yeardley from the bench.

We moved gingerly inside and Yeardley found a chair in the common room. I retrieved a charcuterie board meant for later and set it on the table, and Candace prepared a small plate.

"I'm all right, really," Yeardley said. "Please don't fuss."

"Nonsense," Candace said in a confident voice. "We'll have you right as rain soon enough." I could see Candace's face, though, and it didn't look confident, all creases and worry.

"Is there anything else I can do?" I asked.

"No, thank you," Yeardley said. "I'm sure William should—"

"William should what?" came a gruff man's voice

from the base of the stairwell.

"Poppy's looking for you," Yeardley said to him.

William's eyes shifted to me and lingered for a moment. But as I opened my mouth to speak, he suddenly said, "I've got to call one of the Lone Wolves," and sneaked into the library. The sound of the door closing behind him us left us in stunned silence.

Candace tsked. "That was rude."

My gaze lingered on the space William had just vacated and narrowed to tiny slits. That *was* rude. And suspicious. Excusing myself, I followed him into the small library, easing the lock into place so we weren't disturbed.

"I'm going to give you one chance," I said, puffing myself up with simulated confidence. "Just one. Tell me what you're up to."

As expected, he blustered some nonsense through his beard and mustache, feigning shock, no doubt.

I held up my index finger and shot him a steely look. "Just one."

"I don't know what you're going on about. I'm trying to make a *private* call." He emphasized the word as if I weren't allowed in my own library.

"To whom?" I demanded. "Your imaginary biker friends?"

William's eyes went wide, and he puffed through his mustache once again. "How dare you—"

My hand shot up to silence him. "I have on good authority that there is no Lone Wolves motorcycle gang."

"That's ridiculous," he stammered. "I don't know who you think you are, but—"

I shot my hand out again, and he stopped. "Why the

ruse, William? What are you hiding?"

"Ruse?" he repeated. "There's no ruse." He moved to pass me, but I sidestepped to block his way to the door.

"I know there isn't a gang, and I know you left the group and then returned not long before Randall came tumbling down the stairs into my arms."

He straightened his form. "I had a phone call."

"To your gang?" I asked in a mocking tone. "You rough sort sure do talk on the phone a lot."

He frowned and looked down at the phone in his hand.

"Prove it," I said, eyeing it too, "or I'm telling Deputy Todd about your lies."

He paused for a moment as if weighing his options. I could almost see the gears turning inside his head as he realized that there was no way to dig himself out of this lie. Finally, his shoulders sagged. "You're right. There's no gang."

I crossed my arms and stepped back as he slumped into a nearby club chair. "Why did you lie?"

"I didn't do anything to Randall, understand? I hated the fella, but I didn't touch him."

A slight inclination of my head told him to answer my question.

"It's just that Randall and Everett—those sorts—they're so highfalutin and think they're God's gift. They get a kick out of making the rest of us feel small. And I didn't want to feel small."

"You wanted to feel dangerous." It wasn't a question. The sagging frown and lines on his face, through the mustache and the shaggy beard, told me exactly what his motivation was.

"That bike gives me something I've never had." He turned toward the window. Outside, his motorcycle rested on its stand in my driveway. "It gave me courage."

I eased myself into the matching club chair across from William's.

He bobbed his head slowly, acknowledging a thought that must have come into his head. "I know why that little lady zips around on her scooter."

I shut my eyes and groaned a little on the inside.

"She understands the thrill. The freedom and the power it gives you to be out there with all that horsepower between your legs. You're like a god."

I forced the thought from my mind. "Anyway," I said, "what about Randall? You haven't convinced me yet. Out of all of you, you despised him the most."

William handed me his phone, pouting. "You can check all you want," he said. "If you must know, I was calling my mother. She's been ill lately—she's nearly eighty-five—and I've been checking up on her."

"Your mother?" I nearly choked, snatching the phone from his hands. I scrolled through the timestamps of his messages and calls. Everything matched. He'd been checking on her every hour, it seemed, including the time I had stepped out of the house that first morning.

He looked at me, terrified. "Don't tell the others," he pleaded. "I don't know what I'd do if they found out I was making it all up."

"Well," I said, sighing as I stood up, "I've got bad news for you. I'm pretty sure they already know."

"What? Really?"

"Yes, William." I shook my head and scoffed, surprised he hadn't noticed. "You're a terrible liar." I stared down at this sad man as he crumbled inward. "But I don't think you did anything to Randall. Here's your phone." I held it out, and he took it without looking up. Softening my voice further, I added, "I'm sorry about your mother, too. I hope she recovers. I really do."

"Thanks," he whispered as I closed the library door, leaving him with the privacy he'd wanted.

Fourteen

"UGH," HARPER SAID with a grunt. "This is going to be painful." She frowned down at Mayor Dewey nestled in her arms against her puffy coat, protected from the cold evening air. He'd grown used to being carried, or so the little furry rolls under his chin claimed. Like a fuzzy little prince.

"You'll be fine," I said to her, but worried on the inside. Jim's Founders Club had riled enough feathers, and grumbles of discontent seemed to drip from every Outlander doorstep. As we walked toward the community center, I kept my dread to myself, sure his presence at the SCAT meeting would to cause a ripple or two. "Just act normal. And whatever you do, don't mention Founders or Outlanders or anything like that."

"Yeah, I'm not crazy."

"Who's crazy?" Angie asked as if she hadn't heard.

"Nobody," I said. "What's got you so distracted?"

Angie fretted, tsking at herself. "Sorry, it's just that I've got Bruno Hauser's sourdough on my mind."

"You're really thinking of recreating it?"

"Juniper sourdough sounds weird."

"It'll be delicious, Harper. I just need the right sourdough starter. I dabbled with making my own when I was younger, but after a few, uh, moderate disasters, I gave up."

"What kind of disasters?" Harper side-eyed Angie, who played it off.

"Nothing major. Anyway, I'll need to source the juniper berries at some point. They'll need to be wild, of course, and organic, and this is the right time of year to harvest, so that's fortunate."

"There're loads of them in the forest right now. I see them all the time along my route on the Coastal Road."

"Really?" Angie asked. "I've never paid attention before now."

"Hey, look!" Harper rushed toward the door to the diner as we passed and Dewey meowed his disapproval. A hastily scribbled sign had been taped to the glass from the inside.

We quickly joined her, and I read off the sign, "Outlanders ten percent off. Tough luck, Flounders."

"Oh dear," Angie whispered.

Harper shifted Dewey to one arm and tapped at the sign with her free hand, a broad smile splitting her face. "Ten percent off. Nice."

"It's not nice at all," I said with a scoff. "This is just more back and forth, pitting sides against one another. We don't need name-calling."

Harper's shoulders slumped. "Oh, yeah."

"C'mon," I said, guiding Harper back to the sidewalk. "Mayor Dewey's going to be late."

We hurried the rest of the way to the community center further down Main Street listening to Angie describe her sourdough starter method. It sounded an awful lot like a mix of advanced chemistry and biology, and I gave up trying to follow the third time she mentioned bacteria and yeast colonies.

The lights of the community center lit up through the darkness as we approached. While a crowd could already be seen milling about indoors, a lone figure leaned against the rock wall closer to the street. Charlie. My body instinctively tightened, and I skipped a step.

Angie gripped my hand. "Charlie's very nice, Poppy. Give her a chance. She's come into the bakery a few times already." Angie's voice lowered before adding, "Risking death apparently, the rest of the town would wager."

Harper and Angie pushed me along, and as we got near, Charlie looked up and smile at our arrival. Her chestnut hair was loose and flowing and her cheeks were kissed by a hint of soft pink, a gift from the cold night air.

"Lovely evening," Charlie said, reaching out and giving Dewey a scratch under the chin. He leaned into it and she scratched harder, letting out a graceful laugh. "He's so charming."

Disgusting.

"Poppy," Angie whispered and nudged me, "fix your face."

"What?" I asked, startled. "Oh." I quickly turned my scowl into a smile.

Harper responded, not having noticed my faux pas. "Yeah, this little dude's got charisma. Leaves a trail of melted hearts wherever he goes." She hefted him in her arms and his furry ginger legs flopped in time.

"Hello," I said tentatively. "I'm Poppy Lewis. I run the bed-and-breakfast. That's the big purple house at the entrance to town." I waved an arm toward the Pearl.

"Of course," Charlie said, "that lovely Victorian. It's so beautiful. I really love the color."

"You do?" the three of us responded simultaneously, absolute incredulity in our voices.

She threw back her head and laughed that elegant laugh again, letting her hair waft in the chilly wind. "That's so funny. I take it I'm the only one? I'm Charlie Barba." She held out her hand. "I don't think we've met."

I shook her hand—warm and dry—and mumbled something I hoped sounded like, "Nice to meet you" and not, "Die, you vile temptress."

"I've been told you're fairly new in town, too."

"Me?" I asked. "Uh, yeah. Less than a year. I spent time renovating."

"Looks like you've settled in nicely." Charlie smiled and nodded toward Harper and Angie. "Two good friends at your side already."

"Yeah," I said, perking up. "I guess I'm pretty lucky. This town isn't so bad once you get to know them all."

"I'm getting there slowly. Dr. MacKenzie has been a great help. He's showing me the ropes."

Harper's head whipped around from where she'd been peering into the community center and she stopped stroking Dewey in mid-pet. Angie inhaled in one fast breath and held it like a puffer fish. Her wide eyes shot up to look at me. I was frozen.

"He's such a sweet guy," Charlie continued. "You all have so many quirks and *meetings*. There are so many meetings." She chuckled again, but stopped as she noticed we weren't laughing back. "Did I say something?"

I took a deep breath and reminded myself that she's new and she's not evil and is not after Ryan. "I heard he's very involved with his son."

Angie deflated and Harper began stroking Mayor Dewey's fur again.

"Yeah," Charlie said, "Ethan is really pushing his boundaries. Do any of you have children?"

"No," I said.

Angie let out a wistful sigh. "No."

Harper flinched. "Absolutely not."

A silhouette, dark against the lights of the community center, appeared on the walkway and hurried toward our small group.

"Harper," Beatrice huffed once she reached us, "I am a patient woman, but if you don't get this meeting started right now, I won't have any choice but to leave."

"What's going on?" I asked. Beatrice was usually so composed, and I'd never heard her speak with such shortness in her tone.

"It's Jim Thornen," she said. "He's intent on making anyone not in his *Founders Club*"—she said the name as if it were poisonous—"feel unwelcome. And I won't stay where I'm not welcome."

"Jim." Harper seethed, hissing the name through clenched teeth. Even Dewey sensed her anger and slipped from her arms and quickly set about nuzzling against Charlie's leg, hopeful for more pets, I was sure.

We marched up the walkway and into the center behind Harper, whose stomps would have made the military proud. Mayor Dewey brought up the rear with less urgency, finally joining Harper as he jumped onto his usual spot on the dais.

Harper stared daggers at Jim Thornen, who paid her no mind as he chatted with Lovie Newman and Trevor French, two of the most enthusiastic members of the Founders Club. They wore their comically large Founders Club buttons pinned to the front of their shirts. Lovie seemed to have overcome the shame of her ancestor's bawdy profession and instead embraced the notion that if she had to accept it, then at least she could be a member of the supposed elite.

Jim was speaking in his syrupy politician voice. "I think it's marvelous, Trevor—a noble history, indeed."

"Thanks, Jim. I'm just hopeful my ancestors led this town as well as you did."

The former mayor nodded solemnly and clapped Trevor on the shoulder. "I'm sure they did us proud. It's quite the burden."

Lovie's gray-blonde curls bobbed in agreement.

"Yes," Trevor mused, hinging his thumbs on the straps of his stained denim overalls, "quite the burden."

Harper rapped at the wooden podium. "Are you still going on about that tonsil stuff?" The conversation stopped, and they turned her way. "Why don't you make yourself useful instead of riding the coattails of your great- great-whatever and offer up some suggestions for SCAT. That's what we're here for, right?" Harper didn't wait for a response and carried on. "We've got a long agenda, so let's get started."

We hastily took our seats, and it wasn't lost on the group that we separated ourselves on either side of the middle aisle according to town ancestry. Founders to the right and Outlanders to the left. Pastor Basil, usually amiable and friendly, sat low in his chair with his arms crossed on the Outlander side a few rows behind Beatrice, while Jim sat in the first seat of the very front row on the Founders' side, with Lovie and Trevor close by like fawning henchmen.

Only Angie broke the standard, plopping into a seat next to me, and Charlie slid in next to her. My lips screwed into a disapproving frown, but neither noticed. There was plenty of room to spread out. Why did Charlie insist on sitting right next to us? She must have no sense of personal space. Typical. No consideration for peoples' personal things. Things that belong to no one else. Things that others weren't allowed to—

"Poppy?"

I shook myself out of it. Angie's concerned face peered up at mine.

"It looked like you were about to sick up for a second. Are you okay?"

"Me?" I asked, trying to hide my guilt. "I'm fine." Angie didn't look convinced, but Harper's voice brought our attention back to the front of the room.

"We have some new members tonight. First, Charlie Barba, who has taken over the Treasures of the Coast junk—er, souvenir shop, on the Coastal Road."

A light smattering of claps followed and Charlie smiled and waved a hand at everyone in the room. Who did she think she was, homecoming queen? No one waves like that.

Harper's tone changed as she continued. "And also Jim Thornen, who—"

"Thank you, Miss Tillman," Jim said, standing up to

face the group. "I'd like to thank you all for allowing me to, how do I say this, infiltrate your monthly meetings. As members of SCAT—what a delightful acronym—we must strive to improve the community for all who live here, whether they are founders," he turned a fond gaze to Lovie and Trevor before turning to the rest of us, "or those who do not have the fortunate blessing of town history to draw upon themselves."

Beatrice tsked and Pastor Basil muttered under his breath, but Jim continued, "I stand before you not only as a founder, but as a durable connection between town and government—a liaison with a profound determination to advance the cooperative endeavors of these two entities." He retreated to his seat with a slight bow.

Harper leaned against the podium with her chin resting in one hand. "Are you finished?"

"Yes," he said. "I think that's all for now."

She took her time straightening from her slouch. "As Jim said somewhere within that mess, he's here as Vista County liaison." She considered him sourly. "No doubt a purely ceremonial role. Now, let's continue on with the real agenda items. Up first, the mysterious appearance of a new, shocking shade of blue bubble gum on the sidewalk outside the diner."

"Shelby said it was extra sticky."

"Thank you, Beatrice," Harper said. "We'll need volunteers to scrape—" Harper stopped short as Jim cleared his throat. "Do you need some water, Jim? Or have my prayers been answered and you're just choking?"

He ignored her and stood up once more. "If I may," he began. "While removing the offending chewing gum may clear the sidewalk, it will not address the underlying issues, which are vandalism and littering."

"That's a bit harsh—"

He cut her off again and her eyes narrowed. "We need to call it what it is, a desecration of town property. That said, I believe the best course of action is to catch the perpetrator in the act. Might I propose one valiant resident be tasked with surveilling the yards of sidewalk directly in front of the diner? Is there any valiant resident willing to take on this task?" Jim's head swiveled to scan the room, and I rolled my eyes.

Harper exhaled with an irritated huff. "I really don't think we need to—"

Trevor's hand shot up and he blurted, "I can do that. My shop's right across from the diner."

"Excellent," Jim said with mock admiration. "Bravo, Trevor."

"All right," Harper said, smacking the heel of her palm on the dais, "that's enough. Trevor, you can do whatever you want, but we still need to remove the gum. Any takers? Anyone? Jim, not you? What a surprise."

As much as I didn't want to, I raised my hand. Maybe it was because Harper needed a win. "I'll do it," I said.

"Poppy, thank you. So busy with a house full of guests, but still has the time to offer her services to the town." Harper's stare had not left Jim's face as she spoke.

The agenda rolled on and Jim continued to pipe up with unsolicited tangents. I thought Harper would explode, but she kept her cool until Trevor offered to trim the roundabout hedges because he thought his "tonsorial heritage" would bestow him some level of skill. At that, Harper was undone, throwing her hands in the air and closed the meeting without further discussion.

Harper stalked up to Angie and me afterward as we donned our coats to leave. "If I hear the word tonsorial one more time, I will smack the mouth that says it."

"Noted," I said. "That went surprisingly well, all things considered."

"Yeah," she said with a change of tune and a wink. "I even got some sucker to volunteer to scrape gum."

"That was brave of you, Poppy. I stepped in it yesterday and it's as sticky as Shelby says."

Harper grunted. "Probably Mason from the diner. I think he just got his braces off."

"Well, I know where I'll be tomorrow after breakfast. I don't suppose I can convince you two to help?"

"Uh, I have my rounds."

"Of course we will," Angie said, elbowing Harper. "See you there."

***

A chaotic scene greeted me as I returned to the Pearl, cold from the walk from the community center and tired from the Founders Club drama.

It was Ivy who lay on the floor of the common room with the others crowded around her and Greta fanning the whole group from a few paces away with her dirty apron, as if that feeble attempt could rouse anything.

"What's happened?" I asked, rushing in. "Is she hurt?"

Candace patted me on the shoulder in a motherly way, and said in a soothing voice, "She's fine, just took a little tumble. Our little Ivy's a tad accident prone, is all."

Indeed, Ivy had raised herself to a sitting position with help from Yeardley and William, but her eyes were still dazed and she held her free hand to her temple.

"What happened?" I asked again, removing my jacket and scarf, but not letting my eyes leave Ivy.

It was Olivia who responded this time. "She got up from her chair and then just, fell. Crumbled, really, like she fainted or something."

"I think she hit her head on the way down," Julian said.

I maneuvered my way to Ivy's side, allowing Yeardley to step back, and William and I helped lift her off the ground. "Let's get you to your room, okay? Do you think you can get up the stairs if we help you?"

Ivy gave a single nod. "Yes," she murmured. "I'd like to lie down."

"Greta," I said, turning my attention to the little woman. She still stood apart from the group, waiving her apron with wide eyes, but stopped when she heard her name. "Grab the ice pack from the first-aid, just like we practiced." I waited until she confirmed she understood. "Good, then bring it up to Ivy's room."

We took the staircase slowly, a step at a time, allowing Ivy to set her own pace. There was nowhere downstairs that would allow her to rest in peace, other than my own room, but I discarded that option immediately, knowing the tattered Victorian chair was strewn across my bed and would be difficult to explain away if anyone saw it.

"Thank you, William," I said as we eased Ivy onto her bed.

"No worries," he said gruffly, then added, "Hope you feel better Ivy," as he left the room, shutting the door quietly behind him.

I propped a few pillows behind Ivy's head, trying to make the bed as comfortable as possible.

"You're so kind," she said. "I'm glad we came here."

"Mm-hmm," I mumbled. What else could I say? All the society's presence had done was sow infighting between the townspeople.

"We almost didn't, you know. We almost went to Rambleton instead."

I wanted to say they probably should have gone elsewhere to save us all the trouble, but now was not the time. Instead, I managed a neutral, "Oh, really?"

"I think it was Everett who suggested Starry Cove. It's so nice by the coast, even in winter, and I don't mind the rain."

The door clicked open and Greta scurried in, thrusting an icepack toward me. Her eyes, white around the irises, were anxiously fixed on mine, unblinking.

"She'll be okay," I told her. "Don't worry, please. The look on your face is making me nervous."

"You weren't here," Greta said in a timid voice, very unlike her. She seemed almost scared.

This gave me pause, but I took the icepack and settled it in place against the bump forming on Ivy's head. "Hold it here, okay?"

"Could you bring me some aspirin? I have such a headache."

"Of course," I said, rising from her side. I escorted Greta from the room and closed the door behind me so we wouldn't be overheard.

I looked down at the tiny woman, gray hair in a long frizzy braid, dress and apron wrinkled and somewhat dirty. "I'm sorry I wasn't here," I said. "You're right, I have been gone a lot, and I'm sorry."

Greta eyed me sideways, probably trying to figure out my angle.

"I mean it," I said. "I've been leaving you here alone with all the responsibility. This is my business and I need to be more engaged."

A moment passed before Greta seemed to accept that I wasn't tricking her. Then she raised her chin, crossed her arms, and let out a defiant huff. "Suit yourself."

I stood flabbergasted. "I thought that's what you wanted?"

"Well," she said, eyebrows raised, "I certainly don't need you babysitting me."

"But… What…" I sputtered. "What was all that then?" I waved a hand toward Ivy's door. "You looked like you were about to faint yourself."

"I don't know what you're talking about."

"All right, then," I said with more than a twinge of irritation, "Why don't you go downstairs and brew some evening tea or mix a potion or whatever it is you do around here. I need to get Ivy's aspirin." With that, I left her on the landing and when I returned with the pill, she was gone. *Insufferable old woman.*

Ivy still held the icepack to her head with her one good arm, and a wave of relief washed over her face as I came back through the door.

"Any better?" I asked.

"Not really. Hopefully that aspirin will kick in."

I poured a glass of water from a pitcher on the tray in the corner and brought it to the bed. I traded the cup and pill for the icepack, and she thanked me silently with a slight bob of her head.

It was her wince as she reached for the water that made me uneasy, so I reached for the icepack. "Does it hurt?"

"It's my arm," she said. "I think I fell on it. But it always hurts anyway, that's the problem."

"I doubt an aspirin will dull that type of pain."

"I'll try anything at this point." She downed the pill in one gulp. "Maybe I just need to rest."

"Of course." As I eased through the door, I turned back to Ivy. "Call down if you need anything."

"Thanks." She was already settling down to rest.

As I shut the door and turned back on to the landing, Olivia was there, leaning against the railing with her arms folded. "Is she all right?"

"I think so," I said. "Just in a bit of pain. She thinks she fell hard on her bad arm so I gave her some aspirin."

Olivia cocked her head to one side, looking unsure.

"Is something wrong?"

"Aspirin," she said. "That's strange."

"Not really. It's a pain reliever."

"Yeah, but why not just take the pills she already has? They've got to be stronger than what you gave her."

"What pills?" I asked in mild surprise. I hadn't seen any pills, and Ivy had never said anything to me.

"She keeps them in her bag. I don't think she knows I know, but it's hard to miss when she reaches for it every time she gasps from the pain in her arm."

I stared at the closed door to Ivy's room, wondering, before turning back to Olivia. "And why are you up here?"

She raised an eyebrow at my tone.

"Sorry," I said quickly. "I'm a little on edge."

She considered me for a moment. "I came up to grab a book from my room, but if Ivy's resting, I won't bother her."

I hadn't forgotten catching Olivia in Randall's room, but I had no reason to believe she was lying about this. We stood in a silent stand off before I held out a hand, motioning her downstairs. I followed close behind. Was she really worried about Ivy? I glanced back at the closed door to her room as I descended the stairs. And what about those pills?

Fifteen

I DEBATED LONG and hard with myself before deciding to steal one of the pills. And in truth, it wasn't really stealing, since I fully intended to return the pill once I figured out what it was. Borrowing was a more palpable action, so I *borrowed* a pill.

I made my move during breakfast, when everyone would be occupied downstairs. Leaving Greta to serve, I made a vague excuse and headed upstairs, quickly darting into Ivy's and Olivia's suite without nary a creak of a floorboard. Sure enough, stashed in a side pocked of Ivy's bag was an unlabeled medication bottle half full of small round white pills, no bigger than the head of an eraser. I tucked one into my pocket and made a hasty exit, ensuring everything was exactly how I found it, sans one small pill.

I returned downstairs just as Angie arrived at the back door into the kitchen.

"I brought gloves," she said, pulling three pairs from her bag. "Trevor insisted on giving me ten percent off because I'm a founder." She tsked and shook her head at the notion. "There was a sign on his door, too." She held up her hands like a marquee. "'Poutlander special,' it read, 'Free pack of tissues with every purchase.' Can you believe that? It's getting ugly out there, I'm telling you."

"After Shelby's lunch special, what can we expect?"

"I know," Angie said with a sigh. "It's just so awful to see friends turn into enemies over something so foolish. I think I even heard Mrs. Perez yell something rude to the fish guy. The fish guy!"

"What about the fish guy?" Harper kicked open the screen door and sidled through sideways before it closed. She carried Mayor Dewey in her arms. "Dewey wants to know."

"Oh, nothing," Angie huffed. "Dewey can't help today. He'll get gum all over his paws and it will never come out."

"He's supervising."

"In that case," I said, "I'd like to complain about the working conditions. It looks like it might rain." I leaned over the counter to peer out the window above the sink.

"I hope not," Angie said. "That'll make this job ten times worse."

"But with your help," I said, "it will go three times faster."

Harper grinned. "The lady's got a point."

"Hey," I said, grabbing their attention, "I have to show you something." I pulled the tiny white pill from my pocket and held it out in the palm of my hand. "I took this from Ivy. She's the quiet, waify one with the broken arm."

Angie squinted at the pill. "What is it?"

"It's pain medication."

"You stole her medication?" Angie asked, stunned.

"Keep your voice down," I hissed. My eyes darted to the swinging door to the dining area and common room. "She's been asking me for aspirin for pain all while having these in her bag."

"So what?" Harper wondered.

My lips tightened. "The real question is why."

"Okay," Harper said. "So *why* is this important?"

I stared at the pill. "I'm not sure yet." Closing my fist, I tucked it back into the pocket of my pink overalls.

"Glad we got that settled," Harper said flatly. "Moving on, what's the plan right now? Are we heading to the diner?"

Angie stuffed the gloves into her bag and hefted it onto a shoulder before rounding on me. "Before we go, I need to ask for a favor."

I was stuffing a rain poncho into my bag just in case it rained, but stopped at this. "You sound serious What is it?"

"Well, I have some free time tomorrow and I need to borrow a car."

"No can do," said Harper. "My car's in the shop."

"Why can't you use your own car?" I asked Angie.

She frowned at me, disappointed. "Roy has it, remember? His mother."

"Right, sorry. Of course you can borrow it. What for?"

"Well…" Angie wiggled her fingers excitedly. "It was Greta who first gave me the idea."

"Oh no," Harper said with a groan.

"Her foraged mushrooms," Angie said. "Remember

last night when I was telling you both about the yeast colony I'll need for Bruno Hauser's bread?"

Harper and I exchanged guilty looks. I guess she'd tuned Angie out as well. "Remind us," I said.

Angie's brow grew dark like an angry puppy. She was about as intimidating, too. "You two never pay attention to me."

"Don't get mad at us," Harper said. "We don't know all your big words. What does 'lactose basically' even mean?"

"*Lactobacillus*," Angie corrected with a snap in her voice, then let out a few huffs before continuing. "Anyway, I want to forage juniper berries for my yeast colony."

"That sounds like a giant load of tedium."

Angie huffed again. "You could help me, Harper. It's your day off, after all. Maybe pay me back for ignoring me all the time."

"Ugh." Harper threw her head back and moaned at the ceiling. "How early?"

Angie's eyes narrowed. "Really, really early," she said, emphasizing each piercing word.

"Ugh," Harper grumbled again. "Fine. But you have to pick me up. And don't forget to bring a bucket of coffee. I don't do well without coffee."

Angie grinned, the satisfaction clear on her face.

"Besides," Harper added, "I can't let you go into the woods alone. You're a tiny plump morsel and you'd get gobbled up by a sasquatch."

***

We knew something was wrong once we turned onto the

straight stretch of Main Street, just past the roundabout. A crowd milled in the street outside of the diner, giving off an agitated energy.

"Ack," Angie screeched, "they'll smear that gum everywhere." She bolted toward the group, leaving Harper and me to hustle to catch up.

"I can't believe you are siding with him," Ursula said in response to something I hadn't heard. "He bought those tissues in my shop, you know. Well, joke's on him, because I raised all my prices."

Lovie, full face of makeup and fists on hips, stared at the hardware store owner, scandalized from head to toe. "Is that true, Trevor?"

"Well, nobody else sells them. I had to get them somewhere."

"That defeats the entire purpose," a voice called out. I was sure that was Jim Thornen, lost somewhere within the mass of rain coats and jackets.

"And what purpose is that, Jim?" That spittle-filled question was from Marty Hardy, red-faced and pointing at the former mayor with a sharp jab.

More shouts boomed from left and right, too quick to place any names to. "Yeah, Jim, what about that?" and "Don't you start with me again, or I'll—"

"Geez," Harper said, letting out a low whistle, "what's going on out here?"

"I think Jim's started a riot." I still couldn't see him, but the swirl of activity radiated from the center of the group, and I was sure Jim Thornen was the eye of that storm.

Angie fretted with wide eyes. "Maybe we should call Deputy Todd?"

Harper's eyes flashed. "Are you serious?"

I pursed my lips. "Fine, then maybe the mayor should step in."

Harper took another look at the roiling mob and then to Dewey nestled in her arms. "I'll call Deputy Todd," she said. Self-preservation was always Harper's route.

As Harper dialed the deputy on her cell phone, Angie mumbled next to me in an anguished voice, "The gum. Oh, all that gum."

"No answer," Harper said, stuffing her phone into a pocket. "Oh, well, I tried. He must be hiding now that everyone thinks he's got a family legacy of lawlessness."

"Then Dewey's got to do something about this," I said.

"Like what?" Harper squawked, incredulous. "Claw everyone into submission?"

Frowning, I pushed Harper and Dewey toward the diner. Angie followed us closely, a hand grasping the back tail of my jacket so she didn't get dislodged and sucked into the throng. We soon reached the front door of the diner, which led out onto the sidewalk and street. Shelby was there, standing out front wagging her finger at Georgia.

"Don't tell fibs, dearie," Shelby said. "You've already ordered dinner twice this week from me and asked me not to tell anyone."

Georgia stepped back, mouth working in silent protest, but Lovie stepped in and stared her down. Georgia wilted under her intense gaze and a look of fear overtook her, like a cornered animal.

"Georgia, I'm shocked," Lovie said. "The rest of us have been eating fish every night from the fish stand and you've been feasting on diner food? I smell like a tin of tuna fish and you've been having... having..." Lovie frothed and sputtered and couldn't finish.

"Cheeseburgers and ravioli," Shelby piped in, "warm and delicious."

"Warm and delicious?" Lovie roared at Georgia.

Georgia looked from Lovie to Shelby and back, the whites of her eyes showing. "I just... I hate fish. I couldn't do it, Lovie. I just couldn't."

"We made a pact," Lovie said, raising her voice and turning to the crowd, "didn't we everyone? Founders support founders."

Nods and mumbles of agreement spread through the group, but I noticed that real enthusiasm was in short supply. Their heads were nodding, but their faces looked unsure. I suspected mention of Shelby's food after a week of eating from the fish stand had set their minds to longing for what they used to enjoy freely.

Jim's confident voice called out, "Founders need to stand together for the strength of Starry Cove's future."

Lovie nodded fervently.

Jim continued over the murmurs of the crowd, "Our heritage must be preserved. Every year we lose more and more of our culture and history."

"That's right, dearies," Shelby shouted sarcastically, "nothing says culture like Lovie's house of ill repute."

By the look of shock and horror on Lovie's face, you'd have thought Shelby slapped her. "Of all people," Lovie blubbered, holding back the beginning of tears, "I thought you would understand the power of entrepreneurship."

Shelby didn't meet Lovie's eyes, and she put on her

best no-nonsense face, but the wrinkling of her forehead told me she knew she'd gone too far.

"And what about Poppy's inn?" Lovie asked, gesturing at me but addressing the crowd. "Her guests die of drug overdoses. I know, because Todd told—" She cut herself off and shook her head, "I mean, it's practically an opium den!"

I felt a hundred pairs of eyes home in on me in an instant. *A drug overdose? Opium den?* Harper and Angie looked just as surprised as I did. The toxicology must have come back. Angie was thrilled that Randall's death was an overdose, even if she was too tactful to say it. Her eyes told me everything. I supposed Deputy Todd blabbed to his wife again or, more likely, she prodded him until he spilled the beans. Randall overdosed, that was all there was to it, but something about that didn't sit right with me. I ran my finger over the tiny round shape in my pocket and scanned the crowd for Ryan, but he wasn't one of the faces staring back. I had to speak with him, but this hostile congregation had to be dealt with first. My guests would be making their way to the community center and church to continue their research, and the last thing I needed was an angry mob shouting that I run an illicit drug house.

"This is exactly the problem," Jim snarled, pointing toward Shelby and me. "Our businesses are bought up by outsiders, our homes are sold to strangers, and it's these strangers who bring drugs and other riffraff into our town."

My eyes narrowed as Jim went on, lamenting the direction of Starry Cove's future and the loss of the exclusivity of founding resident families. He'd be well and happy if no one new ever came to this town—*his* town, as he saw it.

"Is my business not welcome here?" Marty shouted.

"Or mine, dearies?" Shelby's words sounded more like a threat and the most vocal shouting of the founders quieted down to an indistinct buzzing.

"Or mine?" came a woman's voice from the edge of the crowd. Charlie, looking strong and poised, but also disappointed, scanned the gathering.

Even though she spoke reason, I couldn't help but think that yes, she was unwelcome, at least by me. But her look of disappointment shadowed the others' faces as well. Marty, Shelby, Ursula, even my own. And the Founders I knew—Trevor, Georgia, and more—there was no happiness in this. "Say something," I whispered into Harper's ear. "This is the time." Then I gave her a gentle push forward.

She looked back at me then swallowed hard and faced the crowd. Readjusting Mayor Dewey in her arms, Harper shouted, "Listen up, everyone." She waited for their attention. "I, uh, what I mean is… Mayor Dewey wants to say, um, that you're all crazy and you need to stop."

Angry mumbles threatened to boil up from the crowd and I watched my friend floundering in this moment. Harper could tear down a bear with her words, but encouraging speeches were not her forte. I stepped up next to her and put a hand on her shoulder. "What Mayor Dewey means," I shouted, "is that Starry Cove is open to all." Harper glanced at me in gratitude and I continued. "Adding new blood is what makes us stronger, and it's why Starry Cove endures after so many years." The crowd had gone silent, and I could hear my heartbeat racing as I confronted my neighbors. "We love this town, don't we? Ask yourself that. Is it because of long dead relatives, or is it because of those who are here today, new and old?"

Jim's haughty scoff broke through the silence. "Our heritage is—"

"Zip it, Jim." Harper hissed. "Or I'll come over there and zip it for you." Jim flinched, looking properly chastised, and Harper nodded, sure that he wouldn't interrupt again. "Go on, Poppy," she urged.

"It's why I stayed here," I said, no longer shouting now that the crowd had gone completely silent. "Because I made friends." I glanced at Harper, and to Angie waiting behind me. "Because I saw this as an opportunity." My eyes wandered down Main Street, to the Pearl then back to the faces turned my way. "Because I saw a real community."

A few of them nodded slowly, then others joined as they considered those standing alongside them in the street.

"It was less than a week ago when we didn't know the difference between founders and outlanders." Uncomfortable feet shifted in the crowd. Faces cast down toward the ground. "And we should be proud, not because of who we were, but of who we've become as a community."

There was silence for a moment as these words sunk in. Then a shout of, "Well said, dearie," came from Shelby.

"We've got the best community in Vista county," came another shout from the crowd.

"In the state," added another.

"I'm proud to be a Starry Covian," Trevor announced, ripping off his Founders Club button. "All of it."

"Me too, of course," Lovie said, curls bouncing as she nodded piously. "I've always been a fierce supporter of this community."

I gave her a flat stare, but let it slide. Now was not the time to hang on to the past.

As the crowd disbursed, neighbors shook hands with neighbors, and several people filed into the diner, no doubt anticipating a warm and delicious meal.

"That went well," Harper said to Mayor Dewey with a grin.

And she was right. I couldn't believe I'd just addressed the whole town and made a case for putting the founder and outlander spat to rest. I took one peppy step toward the sidewalk and my smile faded. Lifting a leg, I groaned at the sticky sinew of electric blue bubble gum adhered to the bottom of my tennis shoe.

Sixteen

I DIPPED BACK to the Pearl to stuff a few things into my backpack, then made my way to Ryan's house. If he wasn't part of the angry mob, he was likely at home supervising his unruly adolescent. His car was parked out front, so I ran my lines through my head once more. A quick glance in the rear-view mirror caused me to cringe. My cheeks were bright pink from the cold air and wisps of my dark hair poked out of my ponytail at odd angles. I tried to corral them back into place but gave up what was a futile effort. Hiking my bag onto my back, I made my way up the paving stones to knock on the front door.

He answered a moment later, looking worse for wear—rumpled sweater, uncombed hair—but he managed a smile. "Poppy, what a nice surprise," he said, and his Scottish brogue even made it sound sincere.

"Hi," I replied in my dull American accent, "mind if I come in?"

Ryan stepped aside and gestured me to enter. "Ethan's locked himself in his room. Thankfully, he has headphones so he can ignore me more effectively by simply drowning out my words of wisdom without having to blast music through the house. It's really quite convenient."

I'd been to Ryan's many times before, but today I felt like an unwelcome intruder. We remained standing in his living room, furnished with a leather sofa and a multitude of bookshelves. I was fond of this place. "Another rough day?"

"Aye." Ryan let out an exasperated sigh. "I don't understand it. It's like he's turned into a monster. Is this just puberty? I don't remember being this bad."

"I doubt any of us do," I said with a light-hearted smile.

"I apologize if I'm doing my best Poutlander expression." He looked at me from behind his glasses with sheepish puppy dog eyes. "I don't suppose you brought any complimentary tissues from Trevor's hardware store?"

"Oh," I said, eyes wide, suddenly remembering the events of that morning, "you missed all the excitement."

"What excitement? Did Shelby finally put bangers on the menu?"

"No, sorry, no bangers. But the founder feud is finally over."

"Finally? That's good, I suppose—no more rubbish discounts. Even though Shelby took ten percent off her prices for us outlanders, she raised them ten percent to offset the loss."

"That definitely sounds like Shelby."

"Well?" he asked, urging me to continue, "Don't hold back—what happened?"

I shared the story with him, leaving out only a few minor details that seemed boastful. It was nice to talk to him again like friends. He laughed in the right places and threw scorn at Jim for starting the mess in the first place.

"I'm glad it's over," he said, then added in a more serious tone, "but you haven't forgotten that I'm Braveheart, have you?" His words could have been joking, but he gave me a look that said he hoped I truly hadn't forgotten him.

I swallowed the lump that rose in my throat. "No," I said, pulling my eyes from his. "I haven't forgotten."

An awkward silence followed, and I tried my best to appear casually calm but in reality, my mind turned in circles. He fidgeted with the stitching on the back of his sofa.

"I wanted to—"

"Should we—"

"Sorry," he said, shaking his head with a half-smile. "You go."

What had he been about to say? He waited for me to continue, so I put the thought aside and pulled the pill out of my pocket. "Do you know what this is?"

Ryan took the small white pill from my hand, our fingertips brushing slightly in the transfer. His hand was warm. Was that a spark?

"Hmm," he murmured, adjusting his glasses. "Hard to say for certain—looks like the imprint has worn off a bit."

"It's been in my pocket all morning," I confessed.

"Where is this from?"

"It's from one of my guests, Ivy. She's the one with the broken arm."

He nodded his acknowledgement. He must have remembered from the town meeting and other events.

"She fainted last night in the common room, and then asked me for an aspirin for the pain. I thought it was just a headache because she hit her head in the fall, but I think it was really her arm that hurt."

He lifted his glasses and squinted at the pill again.

"But Olivia—that's the other young woman staying at the Pearl—she said that Ivy's been popping these every time she's in pain. There was no label on the bottle, either. So, now I don't know what to think. Why would she take both?"

"This could be several things," he said, holding up the pill between his thumb and forefinger. "There are lots of small white pills that look just like this. I'll have to test it at the pharmacy. I don't have any equipment here."

"There's something else," I said. "I think Randall Portsmouth's death was an overdose. Opiates, or something like that."

"What makes you think that?"

"Lovie Newman. The toxicology must have come back."

Ryan nodded. He knew what I meant about Lovie. "This could definitely be in that drug class. I'll see what I can find out."

"Thanks, I'd really appreciate it." And then we were back to that awkward silence. I should go, I told myself, and let Ryan deal with his son, but then I remembered why else I'd come. "I've got something else for you," I said, pulling off the straps of my backpack. A book appeared in my hands and I thrust it toward Ryan with a grin.

He read off the title. "*Carpentry for Beginners. What's this?*"

"This," I said, tapping the cover, "is for Ethan."

"Carpentry?" Ryan seemed confused.

"From the library. It was Ursula's idea. She mentioned her son found woodworking to be a creative and emotional outlet, so I thought Ethan might be interested."

"That's really thoughtful, Poppy. Thank you."

"And," I continued, "you have that unfinished gazebo out back."

Suddenly, he seemed less enthusiastic about the suggestion. "You want my son to build the gazebo? It's just a mossy pile of lumber at this point."

I shrugged. "Why not? Power tools could be a great outlet to channel all that teen angst of his."

Ryan looked at the book, unsure, then back to me. "No promises the book will be returned in good condition."

"No worries," I said, waving him off. "I'm positive the library has experienced graver offenses. Some within the past few days, even."

A loud slam startled us both, and we turned to the hallway, from where the sound had come. Ryan turned back and clenched his jaw. "Just my son expressing his emotions by closing the bathroom door with excessive force."

I tapped the book again and gave a thumbs up. "I should probably go so you can get started on that." I made my way to the door. "Don't forget about that pill."

"I won't," he said, then paused as if he wanted to say more.

I waited a few agonizing seconds for him to speak,

but he said nothing. "I have to ask," I said finally. No more waiting, no more pussyfooting around the subject. "Why will you spend time with Charlie but not with me?"

"Charlie?" he seemed surprised behind those glasses. "She's a friend. You remember what it was like to be new in town."

"What does that make me, then? Aren't we friends?"

"Poppy." His voice was anguished, and he stepped close, taking my hand in his. Warm still. Was that a spark again? He lifted my hand and kissed it gently, his lips brushing my skin. "You are more than a friend," he whispered.

Seventeen

THE REST OF that day floated away, and I spent the chilly day humming around the Pearl, straightening this and dusting that, with little thought to anything else. Occasionally, I'd gaze at the spot on my hand where Ryan had kissed me, and my mind would wander again, all sun and rainbows.

"What the dickens has gotten into you?" Greta asked as she came in the front door. She scowled up at me, helmet still on her head after returning from her daily excursion to terrorize the county library staff. "You look like a brainless chicken."

"Hmm?" I murmured, not really paying her any mind.

"It's nearly four. Have you even put out the tea?"

"What's that?"

"The tea. T-E-A. Tea."

"Oh," I said, shaking out of my daze. "I must have forgotten."

"Honestly," Greta said, pulling off her helmet with a

scoff, "I can't leave this house for one minute without everything going up in smoke."

Now fully out of my daydreaming, I replied flatly, "If I remember correctly, the only time this place actually went up in smoke was when *you* were left in charge."

She waved me off without a glance. "Suit yourself, but you might be a little fuzzy on those details." With a flick of her wrist, she flung her helmet onto a peg of the coatrack in the foyer and flounced into the kitchen.

"Not fuzzy," I grumbled, but let it go and followed her into the kitchen. "How was the library?"

"Violent."

"Violent?" I asked, startled.

"Mm-hmm," Greta mumbled after she put the kettle on. "Moira and I have been re-enacting the Battle of Waterloo."

"What are you talking about? Who is Moira?"

Greta blinked at me as if I were a toad. "Moira the librarian. You met her the other day."

My jaw fell open, dumbfounded. "*That* librarian? I thought she hated you?"

Greta wiggled her nose and scoffed. "Me? Who could hate me?" She continued to flit about the kitchen and piled teacups one-by-one onto a tray with the delicate tinkling of dishware. "Besides, I let her be the Duke of Wellington. I claimed Napoleon, of course. He may have lost, but he did it with style." She lunged at me in her long skirt, miming a few jabs of swordplay with the sugar spoon. "Things got dicey when a child from the after-school program wandered into my light infantry, but we persevered. You may or may not be hearing from an attorney, by the way."

No amusement showed on my face as I stared down at the tiny general with my arms firmly crossed. "You're supposed to be researching Claude Goodwin and his associations, remember?" I motioned in the vague direction of my room. "There's a chair carcass taking up a lot of space in my living quarters that we're supposed to be figuring out."

"Ahh, yes, all that bloody business."

"The blood riddle. 'Only those born of golden blood' yada yada."

"Yes, yes," she said, shooing me off with a waggle of her hands. "About that, Moira said a number of Vista County history books were checked out months ago and never returned."

"Really?" This was a new development, even if it wasn't a good one. "By whom?"

"Said she couldn't tell me."

My shoulders slumped.

"But she could tell Napoleon."

I perked up again.

"Unfortunately, she told Napoleon that the books were checked out by a John Smith—an alias, no doubt—who was quite articulate, from what she remembered."

"That could be anyone."

"Don't be ridiculous," Greta said. "It was a man, so that eliminates at least half the population. We know it wasn't, say, the Queen of England or Nancy Drew."

"That still leaves four billion non-fictional people. I wonder if it was Randall Portsmouth. He tried to get early access to the church records, too. Did Moira say anything else?"

Greta heaved the laden tray into her arms with a

grunt. "I'm fairly certain she did, but I can't quite pull that memory out. It will come back with time, though, just needs to rattle about for a while. Now, give me a hand with this tea. It won't serve itself."

***

We'd finished laying out the tea, and the guests were settling in for a cozy evening by the fire when the doorbell rang. The entire genealogy group was already back at the house, resting after their long day of rummaging through the community center records, or interviewing the fish guy, or however they were filling their time until Deputy Todd authorized them to leave town. The faint tinkling of their teacups dwindled as I reached the door.

"Deputy," I said, greeting Deputy Todd who stood bundled against the chilly night.

"Let me in. It's cold as an ice cube in a snowstorm out here."

I quickly motioned him inside, but we remained in the foyer away from my guests. "I suppose you heard about the near-riot today." I kept my voice low. As far as I knew, none of the group had gotten wind of the dust up from that morning.

"Mm-hmm," he mumbled with a scornful scowl. "Leave it to Jim to—" He cut off with a sharp look, as if I'd lured him into saying more than he should. "But that's not why I'm here."

"Then you must be here about Randall Portsmouth's overdose."

The deputy looked as if he'd swallowed a lemon. "How did you…"

"Lovie."

He muttered something under his breath, then let out a heavy sigh. "Cause of death is official—opioid overdose. And not by a little, mind you. Mr. Portsmouth must have had a real problem with the stuff."

"How awful," I said.

"Fits all the details in your initial statement, too. He must have gone upstairs, popped a bunch of pills, then dragged himself down the stairs once he realized he was done for."

"At least Angie will be glad that her cinnamon rolls have been exonerated."

"I think it's time I spoke with your guests."

"Of course," I said, moving aside so the deputy could step through into the common room. "They're all here."

At the sight of Deputy Todd, each person stopped where they were, surprised, then gathered in the seating area as he motioned them to join him.

"Do you have news, deputy?" Julian asked.

Deputy Todd nodded solemnly. "I'm afraid I do. The toxicology report shows Randall Portsmouth died of a drug overdose. Opioids, to be exact."

I stood apart from the group, observing their reactions. There was general surprise from most, but Ivy went pale and Olivia shook her head the faintest bit and scoffed. "Figures," she said.

"That can't be right," Julian said. "Randall would never take drugs. He was entirely health-conscious. He never drank and stayed away from sugar completely."

"He ate two of the cinnamon rolls," I said, reminding him.

Julian tilted his head, conceding the point.

Candace tsked. "You can never really know what

secrets people are holding."

Yeardley and Olivia nodded in agreement, but Julian frowned. "I still can't believe Randall had any type of drug problem."

William spoke up, "Randall wasn't any friend of mine, but I knew him well enough and I agree with Julian. That doesn't sound one bit like Randall."

"Apparently," Everett said without emotion, "the toxicology report says otherwise." He lifted the teacup to his mouth and took a single sip.

"Now," Deputy Todd said, "since that's settled. You've all been very patient. I know you're all eager to return to your own lives, so you're free to leave Starry Cove."

This caused a minor stir among them before Julian spoke up. "It's already late. I suggest we leave in the morning." There were some grumblings, but they all soon deferred to their leader and nodded agreement. The matter was determined. Greta and I would serve breakfast one last time in the morning, then my grand opening guests would be released from their mandatory confinement.

Eighteen

ANGIE ARRIVED EARLY to borrow my car, just as she'd
threatened. Mayor Dewey followed her inside, took his
usual spot on the kitchen table and meowed for food. The
sun had barely made an appearance through the eastern
forest, a dull, pale ball of orange hiding behind the fog
and dense trees. Despite the hour, Angie was fully awake
and chattered on about her yeast as I wiped the sleep from
my eyes.

"I should get a good haul this time of year," she said.
"Harper said there's a spot just off the Coastal Road
where we can forage."

"Mm-hmm," I mumbled while splitting a pot of coffee between my largest mug and two travel mugs for Angie to take.

"The days are so short, so I want to take advantage
of all the daylight I can."

"Mm-hmm."

"I think I'll start with a week-long fermentation at a
controlled seventy-two degrees. It'll all depend on the

yeast, of course, but that goes without saying. I already have a journal ready to record its progress. Then I'll have to decide on my flour, too, which may be tricky and I'll need… Are you even listening to me?"

"Mm-hmm."

Angie eyed me narrowly. "What's got you so distracted?"

"It's just early," I said.

One eyebrow raised. "You're lying." Her eyes bored into mine, which were still half-asleep, barely acclimated to the morning.

My lip twitched.

"I knew it," she said. "Spill it."

I grinned. "Ryan and I are back."

"Back? As in, back together?"

I nodded, hiding my grin in a swig of coffee. "I went to his house yesterday to ask about that pill and he, we… He kissed my hand and…"

"Oh," Angie tittered, "I'm so excited for you two. You're such a cute couple. And Cesar will be absolutely devastated." She shot me an amused grin.

"There's still his kid, though, so we're back on, but taking things slow. But definitely back."

Angie nodded fervently. "I'm sure his son will get through this phase. Maybe he needs, you know," she glanced up at me, testing my response, "a mother figure in his life."

My mouth went dry. "Don't get ahead of yourself," I said, and she chuckled innocently. "Tell me more about your bread. I'm listening now."

Her eyes twinkled. "I'm going to start on the—"

The kitchen's swivel door swung open and Greta

stomped in. "Shells bells! What's all this racket?"

Angie straightened, brimming with excitement and confidence. "I'm hunting yeast."

"Hmph," Greta said with a grunt. "Here for the gynecologists then, eh?"

"What? No," Angie said, her face scrunching into a pucker.

"Bread yeast," I said. "Angie's going out to collect wild yeast to make bread."

Greta eyed Angie up and down doubtfully. "Suit yourself," the tiny woman said. "Just stay out of my way." She scuffled to the refrigerator, her slippers sliding across the floor. "I had a dream about bacon and blueberries and now I need to experiment."

"All right," Angie said, grabbing the two travel mugs. "I'm off to pick up Harper. I'm sure she'll be pleasant company this early."

"No doubt," I said, grinning into my coffee.

The kitchen door closed behind Angie and I watched her bundled figure disappear from the porch toward the car. "Blueberry bacon sounds awful," I said, staring out at the mist and pale light of the morning. "Everyone will hate it."

Greta rustled in the fridge, pulling out the cuts of bacon and a pint of blueberries, among other things. She cradled the precarious pile of ingredients in her arms. "We'll just see about that."

***

"This is absolutely divine," Candace gushed, shoveling more blueberry-glazed bacon onto her fork. "A magnificent send-off."

Greta glanced at me smugly from the corner of the dining room and I let out a sigh. I should have known she'd make something spectacular. That woman could turn trash into gourmet treasure if she had to, and I struggled just to fry a single egg without torching the whole place. "Thank you, Candace," I said. "It's really all Greta's doing." I ground my teeth through a beaming smile.

"It really looks wonderful," Yeardley said. She gazed longingly at the pile of bacon on Candace's plate, although there was none on her own. "A bit too salty for me to try, but that's bacon for you."

"More for me then," Candace said, clucking into her coffee.

"I'm glad you're all able to enjoy one last breakfast before you go." I peered around the corner of the dining room at the pile of suitcases and bags placed at the base of the stairs. "I see that most of you have already packed."

"We've taken up enough of your time and hospitality." The others nodded at Julian's words, most of their mouths full of Greta's home cooking.

"I can't wait to return home," Olivia said. "This entire experience has been a mess. Not you, Poppy," she reassured me, "but everything with Randall was just..."

"Well," Candace said, "you can doom-and-gloom as much as you want. Yeardley and I are going to take the scenic route. We're headed to that old gift shop up the Coastal Road. What's it called? I can't remember."

She must mean the junk shop Charlie resurrected. "The Treasures of the Coast," I said.

Candace snapped her fingers. "That's it. Treasures of the Coast. Full of knick-knacks and all sorts of fun things."

William puffed out his mustache. "I might run the old hog up that way, too. Meet up with a few of the guys from the gang."

Olivia rolled her eyes, but said nothing, and I tried to stifle a catch of my throat. Everett stared silently into his tea.

"What about you, Ivy?" I asked. "Any plans after this?"

Ivy sat at the last chair on the far side of the long table. She ate silently, still cradling her broken arm close to her body and seemed startled at my question. "Nothing much," she said in a meek voice. "Return home, I suppose."

"All things considered," Everett said, sparing Ivy the attention, "it has been an entirely enlightening stay."

"I'm so glad you were still able to present and share your research with our town." I conveniently left out the part about sparking a civil war and small-town street riot. "And I'm sorry I wasn't able to participate."

Yeardley started in surprise. "I thought you were?"

I shook my head. "I was assigned to Randall, but it doesn't seem there was anything of much interest to report."

Olivia tilted her head slightly to the side. "But I thought…"

"That's too bad," Candace said as Olivia trailed off. "If there's one thing we've learned, it's that every family has at least a little spice hiding somewhere." She let out a hearty snort, and the others nodded knowingly before diving into breakfast once again.

When the time came, it was Everett who was first to

leave, tidily packed and professional at all times. He said his goodbyes with a simple nod of the head, then disappeared into a taxi. It was all a whirlwind as they departed after such an eventful stay, and I was sad to see them go, not the least because that left me alone in the house with Greta for company.

William sped off on his motorcycle, the engine roaring as he left us in the dust, and Olivia was not far behind. She thanked me with a quick shake of the hand, then zipped out the door on William's heels. It seemed she couldn't wait to make the Pearl a distant memory.

"Alas," Candace said in dramatic fashion as she floated down the stairs. "Parting is such sweet sorrow." She and Yeardley showered me with hugs and well-wishes and a few apologies for all the trouble the group put me through.

"It's okay, really," I assured them. "Stranger things have happened, trust me."

"If you say so," Yeardley said as if she thought that couldn't possibly be the case. "Gosh, it's been a week, hasn't it?"

"C'mon," Candace motioned to the other woman. "We want to stop at that shop on the way and all the good stuff will be gone if we keep dawdling. You too, Ivy." The older woman caught sight of the younger lingering at the base of the stairwell. "Time to get a move on and leave Poppy to regain her sanity."

The two older hens clucked their way down the porch stairs, a welcome burst of vitality after the previous week, and I was sad to see them go. Ivy lingered, however, and approached me meekly carrying her bags with her one good arm.

"I hope you enjoyed your stay, Ivy."

"I…" the mousy woman started to say, and glanced toward Candace and Yeardley, whose boisterous voices drifted from the walkway. When Ivy turned back to me, her gaze was downcast. "I think I should tell you—"

"Looks like your taxi's here, Ivy," Candace shouted and waved at Ivy to hustle. "Leave poor Poppy alone. She's had enough of our drama for one lifetime."

Ivy's meekness seemed to get the better of her, and she whispered a quick, "Thank you," before scurrying out the door toward her taxi, never lifting her eyes.

What had she wanted to say? I thought to call out to her, but she was already down the path, moving swiftly past the cackling hens, too far away to hear me. I had never returned the borrowed pill, and a pang of guilt ripped through me.

A thump upstairs quickly left the thought behind. Julian was the last guest to leave, and I hadn't seen him since the end of breakfast when everyone scattered to begin their swift departures. A long day of cleaning lay ahead for Greta and I, as all the rooms would require service, as well as the other common spaces. I called into the kitchen for her to meet me upstairs, then took the stairs to the second-floor landing.

I rapped lightly on the door to Julian's room, although it stood ajar and I could easily see inside. It wouldn't do for me to startle the elderly man. He stood next to the grand, elaborately carved Victorian bedframe, packing papers into the box that once belonged to Randall.

"Ah, Poppy," he said as he turned toward my knocking. "I've been sorting through Randall's notes. Didn't you say there was nothing about your family?"

"That's right," I said with a simple shrug. "Everett wasn't able to find anything in Randall's notes."

"That's odd…"

"Who's odd?" Greta asked, dipping under my arm and into the room. She carried a tub of cleaning supplies and I snagged her arm, pulling her back.

"Clean *after* the guests have left, please."

"Hmph," she said, "Suit yourself." Then she plopped into a gilded chair in the corner of the room, waiting with the bucket of cleaning supplies, filled with bottles and rags, sitting on her lap.

I returned my attention to Julian, who now held a manila folder in one hand. A few loose papers poked haphazardly from the top. "What's that?" I asked, nodding toward the papers in his hand.

"That's what's so odd," he said. "This is an entire folder on your heritage. Randall was thorough with his research, so the amount of information is no surprise, but it's odd that Everett would have missed this."

I took a few steps toward Julian and he handed me the folder. My name—Poppy Lewis—was written on the front in sturdy, block letters, not easily missed. "Have you read these?"

"Not everything." Julian said. "I had only just realized what it was when you came in."

My eyes scanned the pages that stuck out at the top and spied the name Arthur Lewis—that was my uncle. The words and notes that filled the pages were written in an elegant scrawl I assumed to be Randall's, although in bits and fragments of thoughts jotted down in haste. I skimmed the remainder of the first loose page and the names Bethany Pye and Evelyn Buchanan were listed, too, although they meant little to me. I handed the pile of pages back to Julian. "Do you know what this means?"

Julian adjusted his reading glasses, and I waited while he studied the writing. "Arthur Lewis here," he said finally, tapping on the page "is your paternal uncle." I nodded, waiting for him to go on. "And this Bethany Pye appears to be his mother."

"Granny Lewis," I whispered, more to myself than for anyone else to hear. Julian's questioning look made me notice I'd gone silent, so I said, "I think my granny's name was Beth, but she died before I was born."

Julian nodded and mumbled, "Mm-hmm. Pye must be her maiden name. And you can see here." He held the page out for me to follow and his finger pointed toward the faint line that attached the names to one another. "Evelyn Buchanan was her mother. Randall must have been piecing your family tree."

"So, I do have a story," I said. "Is there anything else you can tell me?" I scooted closer so I could read the pages along with him, although he flipped through and I quickly lost track of names.

"Huh," he said finally. "This is quite interesting."

"What?" My voice was eager, excited that I was finally learning something about my ancestors.

"It looks like you had some interesting history after all." He tsked and shook his head. "It's a shame Everett missed this. It would have been exciting to share at your town meeting."

"What is it?" I could hardly contain myself. "Someone famous?"

"Well," he said, dipping his chin, "that depends on

who you ask. Does the name Claude Goodwin sound familiar to you?"

It was as if my heart had stopped, and a small gurgle sounded from the corner where Greta sat. "What?" I asked, my voice shaking.

"Claude Goodwin. He was quite the public figure around here in the early days—a logging baron, very wealthy. According to Randall's notes, Claude Goodwin was…" His voice trailed off as his eyes and finger swept down the page. "Yes," he finally said, nodding in satisfaction. "Claude Goodwin was your third great-grandfather. How about that?" He beamed up at me with his warm smile.

My face was frozen, jaw slackened.

"He's her *what*?" Greta screeched, hopping off the chair. She scurried over and snatched the pages from Julian's hand.

He winced at her roughness, but turned to me and said, "It appears you are a founder after all, Poppy."

"A founder." I repeated as if in a daze. "Claude Goodwin, really?"

He nodded. "You both seem surprised."

"It's just that…" I couldn't find the words. I felt unsteady on my feet.

"It's just that it's a lot of information," Greta cut in, finishing for me. Her steely eyes darted nervously from me to Julian and back again. "Anyway, lots to do around here."

"Of course," Julian said, catching on to Greta's hint and took up his suitcase. "I should be going. I'm glad we found that, though." He nodded toward the papers Greta clutched in her hands. "At least we don't leave you empty-handed." He took up my hand and shook it, but I was jelly. "Thank you for a lovely stay, despite the unfortunate business about Randall. Your hospitality—both of you—has been most generous and reassuring."

"Yes, yes," Greta said in a sickly-sweet tone, her arm guiding Julian toward the door. "Thank you for all your work. We can keep this, yes?" She held up the papers. "Good," she continued without waiting for a response. "Gosh, what a great time we've had, but it's time to go bye-bye now. Okay, there're the stairs. I'm sure you can see yourself out. Bye now. Bye. Bye." Then Greta shut the door behind Julian, leaving the two of us staring at one another in stunned silence.

Nineteen

IT WAS GRETA who spoke first. "I have no idea what this all means, but we've just learned something important."

My mind was still in a pretzel, and I leaned against the bed to steady myself against the wooziness that overtook me. *Claude Goodwin was my ancestor*. How was that possible?

"What about this house?" Greta asked. "I always thought Arthur bought it on the cheap. Has it been in the family all this time?"

I could do nothing but blink at her questions. This news hit me like a train, and I slumped further against the bed. The truth was, I never paid much attention to where the house came from, or where Arthur got the house. My assumption was that he bought it at the time he moved in, back in the sixties or seventies, but questions now swirled in my head. I'd have to pull out the inheritance paperwork. More secrets from uncle Arthur—I couldn't believe it. "I think I need to lay down," I said, grasping at the bedposts.

Greta ignored me, tapping a finger to her chin and furrowing her already wrinkled brow. "This could change everything. I need to put on my thinking cap." Without another look my way, she was at the door and gone before I could say a word.

"A Goodwin all along," I whispered. "But then—" My mind raced back to memories of the Gold Hand— their attempts to undermine me, steal from me. They'd almost buried Harper and me alive. Dr. Goodwin. It all came back to him. Then an uncomfortable thought crossed my mind. Was this mysterious Dr. Goodwin my family, too? That only made things worse. I fell back onto the puffy duvet and let out a groan.

The sound of the doorbell brought me out of my daze and I jumped from the bed like a rocket. "Greta?" I called downstairs. No answer. The doorbell rung again, so I quickly made my way down to the foyer.

"Oh good," Ryan said as I opened the door. "You're here. Thought I might miss you." He wore a sporty winter jacket over his white lab coat, and beneath that a pale green V-neck sweater. He was nothing if not predictably charming.

I quickly tamped down the wild hairs from my pony tail and smiled. "Ryan, hi. I, uh, don't know where Greta's gone…" I turned as if to peer into the kitchen.

"She's out here." He shot a thumb behind him.

"What?"

"Looks like she's doing donuts on the roundabout."

I looked past him to see Greta, zipping around the roundabout on the scooter. She must have rushed downstairs the moment I wasn't paying attention. At least she had her helmet on, even if her hair blew wild and loose behind her in the wind. "Her thinking cap," I mumbled. "Of course."

"Her what?"

"Oh, nothing," I said. "What brings you over here?"

"That pill. I took a closer look and thought I'd walk over and share the results."

With the massive revelation a few minutes ago, I had completely forgotten about Ivy and the pill. Forgotten about everything, really. It seemed so unimportant now, but I humored him anyway. He'd done this research for me, after all. "What did you find out?"

"It's a medication commonly used for hypertension."

The blank look on my face made him clarify.

"High blood-pressure."

"What? That doesn't make any sense."

He shrugged. "It's pretty common, really."

"Sorry," I said with a tired chuckle. "That's not what I meant."

"If anything," he continued, "it's odd that she'd have a dizzy spell, especially if she was taking these pills like you said. They should have lowered her blood pressure enough to prevent it."

"What about drug interactions?"

He frowned, but shook his head. "None that I'm aware of."

"Well," I said with a sigh, "I guess it doesn't matter now. Everyone's gone. Their medication isn't even my business. Oh, look at me, haven't even invited you in yet." I motioned for Ryan to come into the common room, which was much cozier than the foyer near the cold doorway. "Can I get you anything?"

"Some water wouldn't go amiss, thanks." He took a

long look around the room. "I haven't been here in a while. It looks good. I hope everything went smoothly with your guests."

"Other than the untimely death?"

"Right," he said, wincing. "Other than that."

I returned to the common room after pouring a quick glass of water for Ryan. "Here you go."

"Thanks" he said, taking the glass. "Don't let me accidentally take this." He chuckled and held up the small white pill.

But I didn't laugh. I'd stopped dead and stared straight at him. "What did you say?"

"Er," he stuttered. "It was just a joke."

"No," I said, grabbing him by the arms. "What did you say?"

He repeated his words slowly. "Don't let me accidentally take this."

My eyes clouded. I smacked my forehead with a palm. "How could I have been so stupid?"

"What?" he asked. Confusion and a twinge of concern crossed his face.

"Do you have your car?"

"No, I don't…" He stopped. "Poppy, what's going on?"

My jaw firmed. "I think I just figured it out."

"Figured what out?"

"Randall. Randall Portsmouth." I turned to the muted sputtering noise coming from the roundabout outside. "I need to go. There's someone I need to talk to."

"Go where?" He twisted around, worry creasing more heavily on his brow.

"Can you call Deputy Todd for me and have him

meet me at the Treasures of the Coast shop on the Coastal Road?"

"Treasures of the Coast? Is Charlie somehow part of this?"

I squeezed his arm for reassurance. "I'll have to explain later." Then I rushed to the door, grabbing my jacket from the coatrack, and shouted back at him, "Don't forget to call Deputy Todd!"

***

My arms waved high in the air, enough to grab Greta's attention as she made her next loop. The scooter engine quieted and came to an idle as she pulled alongside me and snapped off her goggles with a thwack.

"I was just—"

"Scoot forward," I demanded. "Make room."

"Room for what?"

But I had already swung a leg over the two-person seat behind her and nestled myself against her back, arms around her waist, puffy jacket and all.

"What's going on?" she asked in her scraggly voice.

"I know who killed Randall Portsmouth."

"Who cares? The guy was a pompous know-it-all. And between you and me, I don't think the others liked him very much. Besides, we've got more important things to figure out."

"I care," I said. "And a murder *is* important. We need to drive the Coastal Road. You know the way, right? It's just like going to the Vista Library."

With a small frown, she shook her head. "I can't do that."

"What? Why not?"

She knocked on her helmet with a wrinkled knuckle. "No helmet."

I ground my teeth and seethed. Just like her to turn my rules against me. "Drive," I said, "or this will be the last time you ride the scooter. Ever."

That got her moving, and I almost fell backward as she adjusted her goggles and let off the throttle. My grip on her held, though, and she finished the loop before following my pointed arm, turning off to Second Street, the mostly residential road that spoked off of the roundabout. Second Street turned into the long Coastal Road once it reached the dense forest, and it skimmed the coastline, winding its way to the town of Vista.

The cold air rushed by. My cheeks were freezing and the wind in my ears made me shout for Greta to hear me at all. "Can this thing go any faster?"

Greta gave a curt nod of her helmet and I screeched as we lurched forward. With my mouth partially open, a swath of her gray hair whipped me in the face and into my mouth. I quickly spit it out, wiping the rest away with one hand, the other holding extra tight to the old woman.

Greta drove the road like a pro, leaning into the gentle curves and sweeping arcs of the coastline. Under different circumstances, I would have asked how often she drove this fast, but we needed to reach the Treasures of the Coast shop sooner rather than later.

Greta let out a peal of laughter as we sped along a straight stretch of road that dipped into the forest of redwoods and ferns before reemerging at the coast. I smiled, too. This was actually a lot of fun and I felt a sense of freedom I'd never had driving an enclosed car. Greta's cackling continued as we sped past a familiar sight—my car parked along the side of the road.

Angie and Harper, bundled against the cold morning, foraged from a dense roadside patch of juniper bushes a hundred paces from the car. As the sound of Greta and the scooter passed, they looked up from their work with surprise. I tried to turn my head back at them, fighting against the rush of air, and saw their mouths working silently. They looked at one another in confusion, but Greta swung around a curve and they were quickly out of my sight.

The Treasures of the Coast building soon came into sight along the road. It was a weathered old thing the color of driftwood and seemed small at first, mainly because of towering redwoods surrounding it on three sides. I pointed toward the dirt turnout that served as a makeshift parking lot, and Greta sputtered the scooter to a stop next to the two other cars in the lot. I remembered the newer model blue sedan as one from the Pearl—Candace and Yeardley were here—and the other, a burly four-wheel-drive SUV in forest green, must belong to Charlie. Salty wisps of black hair escaped from my pony tail— without a helmet, they had been free to go wild. I must have looked a fright, but I tamped them down as best I could and took a deep breath.

Greta hopped off the scooter, her short legs dropping to the ground silently, and she unbuckled her helmet. "Are you ever going to tell me why we're here?"

That's when I realized I didn't have a plan.

***

I advanced upon the building with caution, unsure how I would approach the situation once I got inside. Various tagged wares were displayed on the porch, and I remembered Lovie mentioned Charlie had bought the place part-and-parcel from the previous owner's estate, so she would have naturally purchased the inventory, as well. It looked no different than the last time I had been there less than a year ago. Best not to let those memories bubble up.

With Greta crouched behind me, I rotated the lever-style handle and eased open the shop door. The faint jingle of a bell above the door gave away our entry, but the shop was packed with rows of merchandise and no others were visible as I stepped in. The sound of indistinct voices—I thought they were all women—came from the front of the store, but my entry had not seemed to interrupt them. I motioned with a hand for Greta to stay outside and she nodded. It would do no good to bring her along and she'd only get in the way if things went south.

Easing down the first row, I took my steps lightly, and only after reaching the end did I realize I'd been holding my breath. I inhaled deeply to ease my nerves, then peeked around the corner where I could see the checkout counter at the front of the store.

"So much to look at," Candace said. I could see her copper coif bobbed with every exuberant word. "It's like a candy store. I was just telling Yeardley not to let me spend a small fortune before we leave."

"I'm so glad you stopped by. It's been slow going getting this place up and running." Charlie's gently wavy chestnut hair and skin were irritatingly perfect, and I imagined what my scooter-blown hair must look like in comparison. My scowl was mostly for Charlie, but also a bit for myself.

"We just love your entrepreneurial spirit," Yeardley

said. "It's always nice to see strong women fulfilling their dreams."

"We don't want to sound boastful, but we're working together on a book right now—something we hope to publish soon."

Yeardley continued, picking up from Candace's words, "A history of Vista County, especially the early settlers."

"Indigenous aside, of course," Candace said. "Lots of pushing and pulling back in those days. Nasty business, really."

"Sounds like you've both got a story to tell." Charlie wrapped a bulky sculpture carved from redwood in sheets of discarded newspaper. The two must have already made the purchase. "I look forward to the publication."

"It's a long time coming," Yeardley said. "Many hours of research. I'll be glad when the whole thing's over."

I pulled back from the corner of the row. They must be talking about the manuscript they'd been hiding from everyone. All their secret conversations and chats away from the group. I thought my heart would beat out of my chest as I rounded the corner.

Charlie noticed me first. "Hello Poppy. What brings you all the way out here?"

Candace and Yeardley turned, and I thought I saw a twinge of irritation reach the corner of Candace's mouth. Yeardley went a paler shade of white.

"Poppy," Candace said with a faint chuckle, "can't get enough of us, I see." Despite the laugh, there was no humor in her voice.

"You forgot something," I said.

"Oh," Candace sounded surprised, and riffled inside her purse. "Nope. Don't think I did. Thanks for checking, though. I think we're fine."

"Not you," I said to her. "Yeardley."

"Me?" Yeardley sounded even more surprised, and her eyes darted to Candace.

"That's right," I said, taking another step forward. "You forgot your blood pressure medication."

"I did?" Her voice was thin, and she wobbled on her feet. Candace grasped her arm to keep her upright.

I took another step closer. "You aren't feeling light-headed, are you?"

"I think, maybe I…" Yeardley's eyes were on Candace, pleading.

"Look here, Poppy," Candace said sternly. "I don't know what you're getting at, but I think you've gone far enough. Can't you see you've upset her?"

Ignoring Candace, my focus remained on Yeardley. "You shouldn't feel woozy if you'd been taking your medication."

Yeardley's mouth worked silently, but she made no words.

"But you haven't been taking your medication, have you? You don't have it anymore, do you?" My voice was sharp, pointed like a knife at the older woman.

"Poppy," Charlie broke in, "what's going on?"

I held up a hand and Charlie flinched. "Sorry Charlie, but this doesn't concern you." Then I turned my attention back to Yeardley. "You swapped your pills with Ivy, didn't you? That's why you've been light-headed. That's why she's been fainting, isn't it? You from high-blood pressure and she from low."

Candace placed herself between Yeardley and me. "I demand that you stop this, right now."

"You swapped the pills with Ivy then you poisoned Randall."

Candace puffed up, eyes wide and stammering, "You can't be serious. Yeardley would never…"

Yeardley seemed to recede, shutting her eyes and coiling her arms around herself protectively.

"Oh, I know," I said, finally shifting my gaze from Yeardley to Candace. "She didn't do it herself. You helped her."

"Me?" Candace blubbered. "That's absurd. I know it's hard to admit Randall had a drug problem, but this is an absolute fantasy."

My eyes narrowed on the woman. "Ivy tried to warn me something was wrong. She wanted to tell me something as she was leaving. I should have pushed it. She knew. Or she knew something had happened to her pills. They weren't working anymore. She must have been in so much pain."

Candace straightened and set her strong jaw. Yeardley crouched behind her like a wounded puppy.

"Odd, isn't it," I said, "how two pills can look so much alike. Small, white, nothing more than a round speck of a thing rattling around in a pill bottle. To the untrained eye, a swap wouldn't even be noticeable."

"Candace…" Yeardley began to cry behind her. "You said this wouldn't happen. That no one would—"

"Be quiet," Candace snapped.

Charlie, who had witnessed this all, put a hand to her mouth, so I knew she'd caught Yeardley's slip, too.

"Why did you do it?" I asked. "How could you?"

"Don't lecture me," Candace said with a sneer.

"He was a jerk, but he didn't deserve death."

Her eyes flashed. "You only got a taste of Randall. He was a thousand times worse, especially to us." She glanced at the defeated figure of Yeardley. "Every word from his mouth oozed with condescension. No woman could possibly function at his level. We weren't even worth his hate, he saved that for William and Everett and Julian, who challenged him. At least they were men, so he put them on a different plane than the rest of us. We were beneath him."

"The gum on his shoe," Yeardley said through the beginning of tears.

A reflex made me glance down at my shoe and I remembered scraping the blue gum onto the curb with disgust on my face.

"I could only smile through so much." Candace tightened her fists, opening and closing them repeatedly.

My gaze switch from Candace to Yeardley, trying to imagine how these two middle-aged women had it in them to murder Randall Portsmouth. "So that's it? He was a misogynist? We've all dealt with that, our whole lives. What brought you to this?"

This time, Yeardley answered with a crazed laugh. "He thought we were inferior, but he stole our work. All of us. Ivy, Olivia, all of us. He was going to publish his grand manuscript, but it was full of *our* work."

The manuscript… Of course. I could have smacked my forehead. "You stole it back. That's what you've been hiding. That's why you two have been scurrying around, whispering in corners."

"And now we'll get the credit that is due to us."

I shook my head, saddened that it had come to this. "I'm afraid you will, but it won't be what you hope."

Candace's jaw hardened again. "But we will." Her eyes flickered toward Charlie. "It's a shame you had to bring her into it. We could have handled this a lot cleaner if it was just you." Without warning, she grabbed the redwood sculpture and swung it toward me.

I ducked just as Charlie shouted, "No!" and flung herself forward to stop Candace.

Recovering quickly, I grabbed Candace by the hand as Charlie wrestled with her to loosen her grip on the sculpture. Yeardley wailed in the background as Candace grunted, fighting us off with snarls and kicks.

It was a wild scene of flailing limbs, and my vision blurred as we struggled. Candace, although older, was larger and more powerful than me or Charlie.

"What in the…" came the dumbfounded drawl of Deputy Todd from behind. "Stop where you are!"

His words stopped nothing, and we continued trying to wrestle the weapon from Candace's grip. A kick threw Charlie to the floor. With just me against her, Candace spat at me and I flinched, but returned with a final mighty tug, and finally pulled the sculpture from her fingers.

"Stop right now!" Deputy Todd shouted, pulling his gun from the holster at his hip.

"They killed Randall Portsmouth," I said as quickly as I could through my panting. "It was both of them."

"Nonsense," Candace said, wiping her mussed hair out of her face. "These women attacked us and I was only defending myself."

Deputy Todd pursed his lips, clearly assessing the situation. Incorrectly, I would bet. "Do you have any proof, Miss Lewis?"

"I have—"

"She doesn't have to," Charlie said, cutting in. "They practically confessed the whole thing, and I heard it all."

Candace scoffed. "You're clearly mistaken. This is some kind of scam you two are trying to pull."

Charlie glanced up at the corner of the shop, directly behind the counter, then turned back to Candace, a smug grin on her face. "I doubt my new security cameras are mistaken."

Twenty

WHAT FOLLOWED WAS mostly an exhausted blur. I realized Harper and Angie were there by my side, and Ryan, too. Slumping on the floor of the Treasures of the Coast shop, I'd needed a good breather before feeling steady enough to stand. I noticed Charlie had stood up, but her breathing was still heavy, like mine.

"Poppy?" Angie leaned in close to my face and stared deep into my eyes, checking their focus. "Are you all right?"

"What the blazes happened?" This was Harper. "We saw you zoom by, then a few minutes later, Deputy Todd practically blew us off the road."

"Stop exaggerating, Miss Tillman. Authorities have the right of way." The deputy tightened his grip on Candace's handcuffed wrist. With a tug, he guided her and Yeardley outside, presumedly into the hands of the backup he'd requested. "Don't you dare leave before I get back, Miss Lewis. You either, Miss Barba. I'll want a full report."

"We'll be sure neither flee the country, deputy," Harper said with dripping sarcasm. Deputy Todd simply grunted in response.

Ryan knelt next to me and took my hand in his. "Poppy, I'm so glad you're okay. You rushed out, and I didn't know what was going on and…"

His warmth—a lovely sensation. All I could muster was a reassuring smile.

Harper squatted next to me so I was surrounded by all three. "Angie and I rushed in right as you pointed the finger at those two ladies. I couldn't believe we'd missed all the excitement. What happened?"

"Harper!" Angie admonished. "Leave her be."

"It's all right," I said, sitting up a little with Ryan's help. "They attacked me after I accused them of killing Randall." I glanced at Charlie, who stood nearby without fussing. "But Charlie saved me."

Charlie clearly didn't take to the attention as all heads swiveled her way. "I…" she stammered. "I couldn't just let her ruin that redwood carving."

This brought out a smile, and I had to laugh, too, although it hurt to do so. Maybe she wasn't all bad.

"Wait," Harper said. "I'm confused. How did they kill Randall?"

I let out a heavy sigh.

"Just give us the short version," Harper added.

"I believe they stole prescription pills from another guest and poisoned Randall with them."

"So, they just shoved them down his throat or something?"

I chuckled at Harper's question, imaging Candace or

Yeardley trying to shove anything down Randall's throat. "I didn't put it together until Ryan asked for a glass of water."

Their faces remained confused.

"I think they dissolved the pills in the water carafe we put in every room, knowing Randall would drink it. Apparently, he doesn't drink anything except water, and maybe the cinnamon rolls were a little dry." Angie let out an affronted gasp, but I continued, "That's why he pointed at Olivia as he died—she was holding a glass of water. He wasn't accusing her, he was trying to say the word water."

"But how did you know it was them? There were seven other guests staying there."

I nodded, knowing this would be the next question. "The prescription pills were Ivy's—"

Angie cut in, exclaiming, "The pill you showed us!"

"Not exactly," I said. "That was actually Yeardley's medication. If I'm right, Candace swapped Yeardley's lookalike blood pressure pills with Ivy's prescription pain medication when she led Olivia upstairs after she arrived late. She must have snuck into Randall's room and dumped the pills into the water to dissolve. It would have only taken a few minutes. I think Ivy suspected something was amiss near the end, but she wasn't brave enough to speak up."

"That's awful," Angie said. "Why would they do such a thing?"

"They claimed Randall stole their work," Charlie said. "And they wanted to take it back."

"And I don't doubt them," I said. "When I talked to Olivia, she also claimed Randall stole her research. But that's no excuse to kill someone. I think it came down to rage. Hatred, maybe, at the way Randall treated them."

"That's some serious anger," Harper said.

"That's right," Angie said, turning to me with what I'm sure she hoped looked like admonishment, "and you could have been hurt, coming here and confronting two unhinged murderers."

"I know," I said, acknowledging my mistake. "I'm sorry I made you worry, but I'm also glad to have you all—" I cut myself off with a sudden realization, twisting my head to peer around the shop. "Where's Greta?"

The other's looked around too, and Charlie even checked the aisles. I panicked, but Deputy Todd returned, his prisoners securely stowed away, and I groaned at his next words. "Miss Lewis," he said with irritation, "would you wrangle your housekeeper. She's driving that obnoxious scooter in donuts around the patrol cruiser."

***

With the morning's excitement behind me, Greta and I, along with Harper and Angie, returned to the Pearl. There was more I had to tell them, but doing so in front of Deputy Todd and the others was not an option. So we found ourselves seated in my common room with fresh mugs of coffee and a cozy fire to mellow our frayed nerves. Greta, who expressed boredom at my rehashing the story of Julian's discovery of my lineage, chose to service the vacated suites instead. We'd abandoned that work hastily to pursue Candace and Yeardley, so I wasn't going to say no. Who was I to tell her not to do the dirty work if she was offering? Such an odd woman.

My two companions sat in stunned silence as I

recounted the details. Claude Goodwin was my great-great- great-grandfather. The house was… I wasn't quite sure. An heirloom?

Harper's face looked like I'd just told her the sky was red. "Let me get this straight. You are related to Claude Goodwin, the man who stole an unknown amount of treasure from his grandfather's tomb—also your multiple-great-grandpa, by the way—and built this house and squirreled away the rest, leaving a cryptic map hidden underneath the upholstery of his favorite bedroom furniture set?"

It sounded slightly crazy when she put it that way, but I nodded. "Yeah."

"Of course," Harper said, amused, then squinted at me. "I see it now. If I give you a gold tooth, you're the spitting image of that skeleton we found in Atticus Goodwin's tomb."

Angie sipped from her steaming mug with wide eyes staring into nothing. "I'm still trying to process that he's your great—I forgot how many—grandfather."

"Do you know what this means?" Harper asked, a twinkle of evil in her eyes. "It means Jim Thornen owes you two thousand dollars from that unpaid debt." She rubbed her hands together, and a wicked grin took over her face. "Plus a hundred years' worth of interest."

Angie scoffed. "Stop being so petty." Then she turned her attention to me. "What does this mean about our search? Does it change anything?"

I shrugged. "I don't think so. Maybe just strengthens any claim to what we find."

"I don't exactly remember us making any progress on that front." Harper nodded upstairs. "From what you've said, Greta's been using all her time to vanquish the children's section of the Vista library."

"You're right," I said with a sigh. "We aren't any further in figuring out what it means. And honestly, I've been so exhausted from my first full-fledged hosting gig, that I'd put the puzzle out of my mind."

"You deserve some rest," Angie said. "I think we've all had enough excitement for one day."

A few precious moments of silence followed, just me and my friends and a hot coffee to keep me grounded. I should have known it wouldn't last.

"Poppy!" came a call from upstairs. It was Greta. And she did not sound happy.

A quick exchange of glances between the three of us before we dashed up the steps to the second floor. Greta stood in the doorway to one suite, the blood drained from her face. She was not afraid—it was more a look for foreboding. I rushed to her side. "What is it?"

"In there," she said, standing aside so I could enter the room.

Unsure of what to expect, I stepped inside gingerly, bit by bit. The room looked normal to me. This had been William and Everett's suite, and there did not seem to be anything remarkable about its state. The armoire and all the furniture drawers were neatly closed—no funny business there—and the drapes cast open, allowing the meager daylight into the room. Everett's bed had been made, the blankets tucked neatly into place, while William's was disheveled—a metaphor for the two disparate roommates, but not unexpected.

"What?" I asked. "I don't see—" Then I saw it. A small, rectangular piece of paper placed prominently atop the fluffed pillow of Everett's bed. As I came closer, it revealed itself to be the size and shape of a standard business card. Realizing there was no danger in a business card, I picked the thing up, then froze. My throat caught, and I lost a breath, gasping through the shock. A single symbol graced the front, a symbol known to me, and to Greta and the others. The symbol of the Gold Hand.

"I didn't touch it," Greta said. "I called you as soon as I saw what it was."

I turned the card over in my hand and another shock took over my body. A note had been written on the back in an elegant hand.

My legs wobbled and Harper caught me as I slumped against the bed. "What is it?" she asked.

Angie took the card from me and read the message. The fear in her eyes said everything.

Harper snatched the paper from Angie's pudgy hands, and read the message aloud. "A most illuminating stay in a mansion built with a fortune stolen from its rightful heir. Regards, Dr. Everett Ayers Goodwin." Her jaw dropped, and she joined the look of dread the rest of us shared.

I let out a long, deep breath and shut my eyes. "He was in my home," I said, dumbfounded. "This man tried to have us killed." I had never felt so violated in my entire life.

Angie rubbed my arm, cooing in her soft, motherly way to console me.

"Right under our noses," Greta growled. "The gall. And he was in Arthur's library, sitting there reading like a… a… reader. It's all coming back to me—he fits Moira's description perfectly." She stamped one foot. "Oh, that boils my blood."

My hand went to my temple. I felt a headache coming on. "I can't take any more surprises."

And that's when the doorbell rang.

***

We made our way downstairs as a group, like a pack of animals moving in a protective herd. I stood in front, with Harper and Angie trailing close behind. Angie's hand clutched my shirt like a frightened child. Greta brought up the rear. Reaching the ground floor, no one said a word as we stood at the front door to the mansion. The only sound came from our nervous, heavy breathing. Shadowy movement ebbed in and out of sight through the full-length decorative sidelights flanking the door, indistinct and nebulous. It could be anyone. My worst fear told me it was Dr. Goodwin, back to finish the job. He'd pick us off like fish in a barrel, one by one. Or it could be Cho, his slithery henchwoman. She wouldn't miss this time.

Harper leaned in, barely an inch from my ear. "Are you going to open it?" she whispered.

Angie tugged at my shirt. I glanced down and my worry matched her face. "Don't do it," she mouthed while shaking her head the tiniest bit as if the motion would attract attention.

I checked for Greta's take on the situation, but she was turned away, head scanning back and forth, scrutinizing the common room. Napoleon guarding our rear position.

My head whipped around as the doorbell rang again. We couldn't just stand there all day. A collective breath was held as I turned the handle. I squinted and prepared for the worst as the door swung open.

But through the slits in my eyelids, I quickly realized our guest was no assassin. Instead, staring back at me was a woman who could have been a few years older or a few years younger than I, her black hair hidden beneath an elegant wool scarf. It tucked neatly into a three-quarter length black sheepskin coat, complete with furry cuffs and lapel. It was like staring into a mirror at a stylish, wealthy version of myself.

"Too busy to return my calls?" Lillian Lewis asked with a puckered frown, eyeing me up and down. Not waiting for an answer, she added, "I've come to stay awhile. My bags are in the car. Please have your staff fetch them."

"Lily!" I exclaimed, relief washing over me as an enormous smile took over my face. I had never been so happy to see my wretched, back-stabbing sister in all my life.

The End of Book 4

Lucinda Harrison is a writer and crafter who lives in northern California with her two mischievous cats. She is the author of the Poppy Lewis Mystery series.

Connect online at lucindaharrisonauthor.com

BOOKS BY LUCINDA HARRISON

Poppy Lewis Mystery Series
Murder in Starry Cove
Best Slayed Plans
A Foul Play
Dead Relatives